Selected Stories of
Manindra Kumar Meher

Selected Stories of Manindra Kumar Meher

Original Odia :
Prof. Manindra Kumar Meher
Former Head of The Department,
PG Deptt. of Language & Literature [Odia, English, Urdu]
Fakir Mohan University, Balasore, Odisha

Trans-Creation by :
Kalyani Panda
DAV Public School, Chandrasekharpur
Bhubaneswar, Odisha

BLACK EAGLE BOOKS
Dublin, USA | Bhubaneswar, India

Black Eagle Books
USA address:
7464 Wisdom Lane
Dublin, OH 43016

India address:
E/312, Trident Galaxy, Kalinga Nagar,
Bhubaneswar-751003, Odisha, India

E-mail: info@blackeaglebooks.org
Website: www.blackeaglebooks.org

First International Edition Published by
Black Eagle Books, 2023

SELECTED STORIES OF MANINDRA KUMAR MEHER
Original Odia : **Prof. Manindra Kumar Meher**
Trans-Creation by : **Kalyani Panda**

Cover & Interior Design: Ezy's Publication

ISBN- 978-1-64560-398-6 (Paperback)
Library of Congress Control Number: 2023939218

Printed in the United States of America

Dedication

This English Collection of Short Stories is dedicated to my most reverent great-grandfather, Swabhaba Kabi Gangadhar Meher whose personality was an extraordinary blend of integrity and aptitude. I feel myself fortunate enough to have my birth in the family of this legendary poet of Odisha who is an endless fountain of inspiration for me in exposing my soul towards literature the whole of my life.

Preface of the Author

I started writing short stories from my college days. The powerful inspiration behind my inclination to writing was my reverent father, Late Kishor Chandra Meher. The human sensitivity, which is the soul of all my short stories, is the product of his magnanimous contribution.

When the first edition of my Collection of Short Stories was published in 1987, Shri Mahapatra Nilamani Sahoo, the renowned short story writer of Odisha and the recipient of the most coveted Kendra Sahitya Academy Award, had counted upon me and aspired that Odia fictions would certainly flourish and prosper in future with my commitment and contribution. As a professor of Odia Language and Literature I was getting inexpressible contentment by completely dedicating myself in the improvement of my students' creativity and passion for writing. It was since those days that I have been writing continuously, though in a slow pace. I am fortunate enough that during the recent two years, four of my Collections of Short Stories have been published, numerous short stories have been placed in popular newspapers and magazines of Odisha and I have constantly been greeted and congratulated by my benevolent readers for my writings.

Indeed, I am not proficient to create imaginary stories.

My ardent readers must have discovered the depiction of my real life experiences in all my short stories. It is because I firmly believe that my experiences are my real treasure of life. I have never been attracted towards the conventional methods of writing stories. On the other hand I have always tried to express and communicate the pain and pleasure, love and fascination of my life in my individual style involving my innocent subtlety and humility without caring for its standard and significance.

I am not at all a renowned writer that anybody will feel the need and urgency of my short stories to be translated into English. One of my most intimate students Kalyani Panda is well connected with my selfless emotions and attitudes in a deeper lever. So I felt the temptation of requesting her to translate a few of my stories into English and make me feel connected with more number of people globally. My beloved student Kalyani possesses unparalleled dedication, love and respect for me. Therefore, I proposed her to translate a few selected stories, which seemed to be better in content and quality, among the five Collections of Short Stories, the stories published in newspapers and magazines and a few unpublished stories written by me. She accepted my request joyfully. After that she made me amazed, animated and indebted by translating my stories one after another with her high-spirited dedication, hearty involvement and selfless attachment.

It fills my heart with immense pleasure and pride that my loving student, Artist Jayanta Kumar Mahattam deliberately took the responsibility of beautifying the pages this book with striking and content-based line sketches. I thank him from the depth of my heart for his valuable support and cooperation.

I extend my sincere gratitude to renowned poet Shri Satya Pattanaik, the Manager of Black Eagle Books for his praiseworthy attempt to propagate Indian literature across the globe.

If a single element of my stories in this book can touch the heart and soul of anyone, my negligible effort will be certainly fruitful.

With humble regards

Manindra Kumar Meher

From the Pen of the Translator

We come across a variety of people throughout our life. Some of them remain connected with us for a very short period of time and fail to influence us much whereas some other remain connected with us in our emotional level and though they stay far away from us, they remain attached with us forever. Such people make our life meaningful, resourceful and prosperous through their perennial love, inspiration and guidance. Such a personality is Dr. Manindra Kumar Meher, my reverent Odia teacher and a torch bearer in my small world of literature.

From my school days I had discovered in me a strong attachment and interest towards Odia language and literature. I was reciting the poems of my Odia books so emotionally and enthusiastically that I could memorize them automatically. Some of the poems are still fresh in my memory lane.

When I studied at Barpali College, I came in contact with my favorite Manindra Sir who was a lecturer there. He was taking the classes of compulsory M.I.L paper. From the first class itself I was mesmerized with his clear and correct pronunciation of Odia words, wonderful sentence construction and heart touching presentation of different chapters. Later on I could discover his multifaceted personality in many other spheres. His deep attachment with the students, relentless efforts to expose their innate potential and his enthusiastic approach to build human beings in class room became exemplary for me. His outstanding oratory skill in various functions and occasions inspired me to learn from him and participate in debate and poem recitation competitions.

When I was promoted to graduation, I was deprived of the pleasure of attending the classes of my Manindra Sir as I opted English as my Honours subject. Yet my craziness and eagerness to listen to him forced me to attend a few classes of Odia Honours whenever I was having a leisure period in my time table. Gradually, I became an active member of the college wall magazine "Basanti" which was the brain child of Manindra Sir. He started stimulating me to narrate my real life experiences in the form of prose, poetry and short stories for the publication in Basanti. I was really thrilled when I could discover my first article reflected on a colorful and picturesque background of Basanti and the readers enjoying and appreciating it. The constant motivation and admiration of Manindra Sir amplified my confidence and acted as a booster to write more and more. In this way I started writing. Starting from my graduation till date, I have written a number of articles both in Odia and English But it was beyond my imagination that I could ever been able to write a book.

It was 27 March, 2022. Manindra Sir requested me to translate a few of his short stories into English. At that time I really did not know that I could do it. In fact, I felt myself incapable of translating the classic creations of such a renowned and versatile writer like him. But when he assured me about my potential and became hopeful of a fruitful outcome, I was determined to fulfill his wish to the best of my capacity as an obedient and sincere student.

While translating the stories, I felt as if Manindra Sir was standing behind the podium of a class room of Barpali College and narrating before me his unforgettable life story and as a devoted and passionate listener I was sitting on a bench in front of him. When I was shaping his real life experiences and sketching his real characters, every time I realized that my heart was automatically connected with his soul and could understand his simplicity, humility, compassion and emotional bonding with others from a deeper level.

At present I am working at DAV Public School, Chandrasekharpur, Bhubaneswar. From the tightly packed schedule of the school whenever I found some leisure time, I engaged myself in translation work. It gave me divine pleasure and absolute satisfaction when I completed my work and surrendered it at the feet of my teacher.

The 17 stories enlisted in this book in English version have been originally written in Odia by Manindra Sir. All these short stories are enriched with their own colour, beauty, splendor and charm. One thing that is common about most of his stories is that they are not imaginary; rather, they have been born out of his personal experiences, day-to-day happenings and deep attachment and insight towards the people living in and around his real life. His characters are also not fictional but the living images of actual life. May it be the ghost of Vijaya who had interacted with him after committing suicide in the hostel room of Sambalpur University, may it be the old lady who was driven out of the bus for her inability to pay the bus fare of one rupee and fifty paisa or may it be Jayanta who was more than a son for the author and his wife or may it be Mani Maa or sister Manaswini who had influenced, shaped and enriched the author's life with their magnanimity and love--every character has been portrayed by him with subtle details, deep attachment and transparency. Most of his stories are packed with the delicacy of selfless and unconditional relationships, the value of powerful feelings and overflowing emotions in one's life to build a lovely and sweet bond with others - may it be human beings, birds, animals or natural objects.

I feel myself extremely honored and privileged of having the opportunity to come across the memorable events that have really happened in the life of my adorable teacher and the unique persons who have constantly motivated and influenced him to refine his fortitude and personality. I extend my heartfelt and warm gratitude to him for providing me the much needed guidance as well as motivation to start and complete this translation work. It was, indeed, a training ground that brought new learning opportunities for me. I am indebted to him forever for his constant love, care and blessings.

I extend my deep gratitude and reverence to Dr. K.C. Satapathy, the Founder Principal of DAV Public School, Chandrasekharpur for providing me a favorable ambience and inspiring me constantly for the exposition of my literary flair.

I am greatly elated to express my deep thankfulness to popular Artist Mr. Jayanta Kumar Mahattam, my dear spouse, for enhancing the beauty and vivacity of this book with the lovely strokes of his pencil, color and brush.

I take the privilege of extending my sincere

thankfulness to Black Eagle Books for shouldering the responsibility of publishing this book and being instrumental to make it accessible for all the book lovers and fans of my teacher across the globe.

May the name of my teacher shine like a dazzling star in the sky of literature. May he touch the zenith of success. May he lead a peaceful life with good health and happiness. This is my humble prayer to the Almighty.

With deep regards

Kalyani Panda

CONTENTS

The Rain

Another shower of rain came. It came like a thief from the morning, drenched the whole Jyoti Vihar and disappeared ensuring the possibility of coming again in some unpredictable time. All trees looked refreshed and vibrant with clean green leaves. The branches hanging in the gentle breeze seemed inviting the rain again.

A cluster of high dark mountains in the southern-west was enveloped with a thick layer of fog.

Pravat did not remember when he came out of his hostel and reached the out- stop. He also did not remember what the purpose of coming to the out-stop was. All the roads were deserted and entirely wet in rain.

There again came a thin shower of rain.

Pravat was enchanted with the gentle and chill pat of rain. He was fascinated with the wave of pleasant wind. He was absolutely thrilled and mesmerized with the sweet melody of a tune floating from an unknown region.

Rain dribbled continuously.

His attention was drawn towards a young girl who was coming from the front. The girl was entirely drenched. She stood waiting for someone under the Gold Mohur tree.

Pravat felt as if the melodious tune, which was repeatedly reverberated in his heart, touched its pitch and mingled in the body of the girl slowly. From that moment his eyes stuck up on her youthful stature.

The girl in her fair complexion was looking vibrant in a navy blue saree. It was as enthralling as the amalgamation of the Ganga and Yamuna. Suddenly Pravat realized that the girl was Shubhra.

The green leaves of the tree were pouring their intense love on Shubhra as if she was a close acquaintance

of a long waiting. One after another they descended and were stored on the dense hair of Shubhra. From there they rolled down upon her charming body. Her wet saree was cemented on her well-structured body and her youthful figure was clearly noticeable. With blushing eyes she gazed at the swelling clouds in the western horizon being engrossed with a deep sensation. She was ornamented with bashfulness from head to feet.

Usually when rain drops fell, that sight used to flash Pravat's memory lane tinkering its curtains.

❖   The rain drops rolled on the patches of green tender grass of the large pasture with ecstasy. There were seven Gold Mohur trees standing in a row. They were all smiling pleasurably. The boy in half pant and white half shirt and the rosy little girl in a navy blue frock were jumping beneath the trees.

The rain was dancing in the entire field. It was dancing on Pravat and Shubhra beneath the Gold Mohur trees. It was dripping down and down in tiny narrow lines. Both of them were dancing in the tune of the song they were singing together entangling each other's hands. They were wetting themselves in the stream of rain.

❖   All the students were instructed frivolously to reach school from the morning to complete the decoration work for Ganesh Puja. However, that morning was accompanied by erratic wind, heavy rainfall, flashing lightening and violent thunderclaps. The Peepal tree in front of Pravat's house became crazy that day. Abiding the instruction of the teacher Pravat ran to school. Standing on the school veranda the teacher remarked, "Why did you come in this rain? Go home.

I'll send for you if required."

Pravat stared at the teacher's face constantly without any movement. He had abundant eagerness to go inside and participate in the decoration. However, he returned home as per the desire of his teacher. White water drops of the heart of the clouds oozed out and rolled down on the earth through his eyes.

He was stepping forward slowly in a lethargic way. He noticed Shubhra coming towards him. She wiped away the white tear drops from the eyes of Pravat in her tiny fingers and took half of it to her own eyes. The teardrops released from their eyes befell on the earth and mixed with the stream of rain. Both of them held each other's hands and stepped out towards their own green world leaving behind the trifling matters of the normal world.

❖   One day they had to spend the night on the portico of the school due to the heavy rainfall from the evening. It became thinner from the third phase of the night. From that time it started singing its pattering song. Being overwhelmed both of them were listening to the melodious rendition of rain embracing each other in that sleepless night. All other classmates were lost in deep sleep. Rain was thumping on the roof of the school. The cold drops of overflowing water touched them gently.

They returned home in the morning.

Rain was showering lightly.

The morning of that day was also the same. From the third phase of the night the anklets of rain were jingling in the heart of Pravat. The fascinating morning song was creating rhythm in his interior core.

Suddenly the bus stopped at the out-stop. The girl under the Gold Mohur tree left the place and boarded the bus hastily. The bus moved forward leaving behind a gust of black smoke.

Someone pulled the shoulder of Pravat. He turned back. It was Manas. He asked curiously, "Hey Pravat! What're you doing here in this early morning? I stayed in Sambalpur yesterday night."

Pravat was silent and motionless. He had just fixed his eyes on the bus delightfully.

"What're you looking at?"-asked Manas.

"Looking at Shubhra", Pravat answered gripped with emotion.

"Who is Shubhra? No one is here."

"She was there but she boarded the bus and went away."

"Bus! But.......... I got down from the bus alone here. Nobody was there. I am pretty sure. None entered into the bus either. Let's go to our room dear. Don't waste your time in day-dreaming."

Pravat snorted at the answer of Manas.

It was raining. The road was covered with pearl-like raindrops. That sweet and melodious tune reverberated in the heart of Pravat. The soft cold touch of rain enraptured him. He felt as though Shubhra was descending on him in the form of raindrops.

(Published in "Ankur" –issue of May-June 1984)

****

Mani Maa

When I suffer from fever and lie down in my bed, I often remember those who are very close to my heart. The people who have made my life resourceful with the charity of their love, their magnificent personalities mesmerize me again and again. Their images often peep inside my inner heart which throbs and pounds with their fresh memories.

Today I am suffering from a mild fever and I am silently lying in my bed. That's why I am repeatedly recalling Mani Maa. My heart has been churning sharply with the memories of Mani Maa from the last few days. Her affectionate motherly image is emerging before my inward eyes again and again. I am so unfortunate that I could neither remained present nor could have a glance of the affectionate eyes of that adorable mother during the last moments of her life.

It is very difficult to define and describe why sometimes we are irresistibly tempted to establish a mysterious relationship with some specific persons who come to our life. Mani 'Maa' is not my biological mother but why she had stored so much love and affection for me in her heart, why she had magnetized my inner self towards herself, I cannot estimate. When I think over this matter, I cannot find any reason.

I strongly believe that if human life becomes

meaningful in this world for any reason, that is for this selfless attachment. If the people, who break down thinking life to be worthless, feel the magnanimity of this selfless attachment fully, then at least they can understand easily how this unconditional loving relationship has made their life fascinating.

Only I know how much hopeless and helpless I was thinking about my worthless life. Only I can feel how much despondent my heart has become while searching for the true meaning of life. But, indeed, my life has become meaningful for those who have enriched it with the donation of their profuse love and affection. Only for them the earth seems new to me every day.

The intense love of Mani Maa has not only created a strange sensation in me but also it has mesmerized me with its magnetic attraction.

I have no idea exactly at what time Mani Maa's auspicious sight fell on me after my birth, but I have heard from my parents that whenever she saw me, she was exulted with a ripple of emotion which could be clearly reflected on her face and in her words.

I keep in mind those days when I used to stay with Mani Maa up to midnight. I would listen to various stories from her. I don't remember what else she used to tell me, but I slept peacefully in the lap of that benevolent mother. They resided near our residence. When I slept in the lap of Mani Maa, her husband, (my elder father) also sat nearby. I was continuously drenched with the tide of emotions that flowed from their eyes and faces always. How happy they were! My inner self did not want to give up their attachment and grace in my childhood. They had only one daughter, Manju whom I called elder sister. We both used to play and listen to the stories together. After that we used to sleep. When I was in deep sleep, my father used to come to Mani Maa's house to take me back home. He usually came after completing all his work for the day. But I was not interested to go with father disturbing my sound sleep. I have heard Mani Maa saying many times, "You tell your father that you will not go with him and stay here only." My father would smile and then come home taking me.

Sometimes the nights of summer seem full of dreams. I, sister Manju, my elder father and Mani Maa-all used to sleep on the verandah. I loved to behold the shining stars in the sky lying in my bed. It was, indeed, in that ambience that I experienced the glee of beholding stars for the first time.

The blue sky looked so beautiful! The dark complexion of Mani Maa mingled with the darkness of the night. I could not distinguish between Mani Maa and the dark night as though the dark night had become Mani Maa for me.

Today, when I recall that serene face so intimately, my entire body is thrilled with a transcendental feeling. As I observe, the root cause behind my deep attraction towards Goddess Kali is a strange experience of my life. The intense devotion of Ramakrishna Paramahansa towards his mother had stirred my tender heart with an extraordinary throbbing. It had made my eyes tearful. His eager utterance of 'Maa' had created in me the curiosity of having a glance of Maa. When I was small, I was scared of "Kali Temple" of Barpali but when I grew up I wanted to behold the serene aura of that loving mother entering into the temple. After that when I got an opportunity to see the Idol of Dakshineswar Kali, at that time I could communicate my feelings so smoothly with that lively deity. Today I know consciously that the face of Mani Maa has all resemblance of Goddess Kali. I cannot see any difference between both the images. When I remember Mani Maa's face, I find the face of Maa Kali reflected on it. When I remember Maa Kali, I find the face of Mani Maa illuminated on it.

Mani Maa was very amicable towards me but she was also not less ferocious. She used to raise her voice against the slightest inhumanity and injustice. The way Goddess Kali terrorizes the inadequacies of human beings with her flowing red tongue, similarly, Mani Maa could make the opposite and negative elements weaponless and rootless with her reddish eyes as well as swift and sharp voice. I have heard the wallop of her thunder-clapping sound many nights. But I was never afraid of her. The way Goddess

Dakshineswar Kali stares at her devotees with her flowing red tongue in the temple, Mani Maa would appear the same if she protruded her tongue.

Her life was a strange one. She had not formed her family in a typical way. I came to know about it from the incidents that occurred in a number of feasts organized in our house. When her husband or my elder father came to the venue of the feast, other people of our caste disliked sitting near him or those who were already in their seats, would stand up and leave the place. Such incidents had ignited the fire of revolution in my adolescent mind. When I tried to unearth the reason behind it, I came to know that Mani Maa was the daughter of a 'Gouda' family. They were maintaining their livelihood with the earnings from a betel shop. My elder father was going to that betel shop everyday for buying betel. It was in this way that the seed of love germinated and grew in their hearts. People started saying that the Gouda girl hypnotized my elder father. That rumor grew more and more but it could not shake their strong bond of love. Both of them were finally united with the shackle of marriage and were exploited with the bitter criticisms and social restrictions of casteism throughout their life. When I saw the insulting behavior of the people of our caste towards my elder father at the venue of feast, I found my inner self revolting profusely. I wanted to tell those people, "My elder father will sit here and eat. If you don't like to sit with him, you may leave the place."

I remember sister Manju got married when I was reading in high school. At that time Mani Maa, sister Manju and my elder father had to go through tremendous mental trauma. Food was prepared for hundreds of people who were cordially invited to the marriage but as usual the social restrictions stood as an obstacle on their way. How could they attend the function of someone who was outcaste? God knows who named caste as 'Ganga'! Does the flow of pious Ganga differentiate among the human beings of various castes? Never! She rather gives new life to everyone with her sacred touch. Then why that magnanimity and openheartedness can't be found in the people of a caste? Why is the stream of caste Ganga so polluted and narrow-mined?

Nobody attended the feast of sister Manju's marriage. The matter reached to the ears of my grandfather. His heart was free from all narrow-mindedness and boundaries. He was very liberal. He instructed all the family members of our house to attend the marriage function of sister Manju and we did accordingly. later on, I heard that after we all reached Mani Maa's house to attend the function, the stream of caste Ganga also started flowing towards the same direction of Mani Maa's house.

We left our old house after our new house was ready outside our lane. Now I was deprived of the opportunities of spending more time in Mani Maa's house. In the deserted afternoons and evenings my heart was pounding with the memories of Mani Maa and sister Manju. So during such moments of seclusion I rushed to our old lane without informing anything to anyone of my family. From the time of sunset I used to remain in the house of Mani Maa till late night and was fully engrossed in playing different games with sister Manju and other boys of the lane in the open space in front of their house. Just like a drunkard I used to forget every other thing at that time.

Today, I cannot estimate why the eyes and faces of Mani Maa as well as sister Manju were filled with such warmth and happiness when they found me playing? I think, all children are same and while playing they move their hands and feet quite enthusiastically. All speak the same things only but why my words, my style, my gestures and movements could bring so much of brightness, contentment and joyousness on the faces of Mani Maa, Sister Manju and my elder father, I was unable to understand. Indeed, I was dragged towards them because of the amount of happiness reflected on their faces after my arrival. When I did not retreat home till late night, my mother or father or uncle used to come to Mani Maa's house to fetch me.

When I was getting anything new, like a new shirt or a new bag, I ran to Mani Maa's house to show it. How cheerful she was to see all those new stuff! She would describe sensitively how handsome and smart I was looking in that new shirt or bag. She would describe me in the same style as mother Yashoda would describe the beauty of Srikrishna. She was enveloped with a divine engrossment while doing so. I was greedy to feel that divine thrill and sensation again and again in my life.

Once, a friend of my father brought a pair of wooden shoes for me. I went to Mani Maa's house wearing the same in the afternoon. Being a mere eight or nine years old boy when I walked on the road with the wooden shoes, I could draw the surprise attention of many people. Kids were laughing at this scene but still my aim was to express my new experience of wearing wooden shoes before Mani Maa.

Once, when I was in Std. VII or VIII, I went to the old market of our lane in my bicycle to purchase vegetables. Mani Maa was also sitting in that market to sell vegetables. I was reluctant to purchase vegetables from her lest she would refuse to accept money from me. Yet, many a times she would call me herself and fill my bag with vegetables. She would be amazed discovering me in the market and advice me to go home carefully in my bicycle. But, frankly speaking, I was not at all interested to return from our old lane. From the market I used to go to our old residence and from there I would reach Mani Maa's residence. I would meet there sister Manju and elder father who would ask a number of questions related to purchasing vegetables. My friends usually spilled out of the nearby houses to meet me and in this way I got to spend another hour of unforgettable ecstasy.

As I grew older, the frequency of visiting to Mani Maa's residence naturally decreased but it could not decrease either my fondness for Mani Maa or her love for me. When she used to come across me, she would address me with so much of warmth and joy. I could feel her amorous embrace encircling me and the shower of affection drenching me altogether. I could not speak much due to my coyness but she would get inexpressible delight even from the one or two words that I would utter. Her eyes would be illuminated with such brightness as if she was beholding something costlier than diamond, sapphire, pearl or ruby. When I remember that brightness of her eyes, I feel the brightness of diamond, sapphire, pearl and ruby to be diminishing before it. What a magnetic attraction she had in her look! Her affectionate glance could drench my face with thousand of kisses. Her auspicious hand would spread on my entire body. Every time she would meet me, she would be equally amazed, equally excited and equally emotional.

After passing from the school, I studied in the college of our village for two years. Then I completed my higher study outside our village. At that time I could not meet Mani Maa frequently. But I remembered her in every rapturous moment. When I was staying in the hostel of Jyoti Vihar, I used to enjoy the setting sun through the window of my room and remember my sweet Mani Maa. Similarly, on my birthdays, I used to be obsessed with the cherished memories of the past and the affectionate faces of Mani Maa and sister Manju would flash upon my inward eyes. Every night I used to write about them in my diary with a steady mind. But most of the time I felt myself unfulfilled and discontented remaining away from that priceless love. Today also I have the same feelings.

Very often my mind is stirred with numerous memories of the past. I did not understand how each vein of Mani Maa's heart was closely connected with my life. Probably I was reading in Std. II in those days. In our old house I was going to the toilet crossing the backside road. I noticed that a mother dog had begotten three/four puppies and was sitting watchful on them. Whether I was afraid of the dogs or not I cannot recall exactly but, when the mother dog saw me, she barked loudly and rushed towards me. Not only that, she also bit my leg instantly. Being terrified I shouted and cried bitterly. I could feel the vibration of my shouting and cries but immediately my interior core started trembling with the vibration of a sound of worry and anxiety that reached to me as swiftly as the lightening from a house on the other side of the road. That was the sound of my caring Mani Maa, "Oh my God! The dog has bitten my son", with this cry she rushed towards me. She emerged by my side to save me as Lord Srikrishna had saved the elephant from the crocodile. Immediately, I felt secured within the ring of fearlessness. I cannot imagine the exact distance between my shouting and Mani Maa's approach as a lightening. It amazed me how the door of her heart was always open towards me. As the heart of the Almighty melts away with the pathetic cry of his passionate devotee, similarly, my helpless cries dragged Mani Maa towards me instantly. The more I remember that incident today, the more the delicate wires of my inner self tremble. When I brood over the incident, even I am sensitive towards that mother dog that bit me that day. Probably she attacked me being apprehensive of the approaching danger for her newly-born kids. Where was her fault in biting me? She was frantic to keep her offspring safe. Today the agony of that mother dog and the anxiousness of Mani Maa vibrate my heart equally. In their frantic attempts to save their children from danger, the magnanimity of a motherly heart is reflected only. When I recall that incident I can have a little understanding of how deeply the tender veins and arteries of children are connected with the internal pulse of a mother.

Sister Manju was the only child of Mani Maa. She considered me her brother. Sometimes she would take me to a nearby pond named 'Karamuda' for a bath or on some other days she would drench me in rain. My body could not tolerate much water. So my grandfather would express his dissatisfaction finding me either bathing or wetting much. Even so, sister Manju did not miss the opportunity of making me swim in the water of 'Karamuda'. Most of the time raindrops were falling incessantly and I used to spend maximum time in the house of Mani Maa. Sister Manju would sit in a charpoy in the kutcha verandah and sing all the poems of her Oriya literature book. I would be found sitting beside her completely absorbed in her sweet melody. It was from those days that I found Oriya literature book to be full of life. The magic and music of that book could reach to my ears sweetly through the melody of sister Manju. The song of rain and the song of sister Manju have the same rhythmic effect in my heart even today.

Sister Manju kept fasting for my progress and success. When she became grown up and we shifted to our new house, she kept "Bhaijuintia" (fasting for brothers) for me. She would come to our house in the early morning of the next day of Durga Puja to tie the 'brat' or sacred thread around my wrist and break her fast. I am the only child of my parents. So I have received enough affection from everyone. My elder sisters, the daughters of my elder father, also kept fasting and tied 'brat' around my wrist. But when they found sister Manju reaching our house in the early morning, they became worried and jealous. They would drag me hurriedly to an inner room if I was found sitting beside sister Manju and tell me, "Why should you allow an outsider to tie 'brat' in your hand before your own sisters do? First we'll tie and break our fasts and then whosoever wants, can do the same." I was nearly in tears when they called sister Manju an outsider. I loved her as much as I loved the daughters of my elder father. So without uttering a single word I again came back to sister Manju. In fact, she was keeping Durgastami for other two/three boys of our lane too. Due to that some of our relatives commented that she was doing a business in the name of fasting. She was thought to be greedy of getting new clothes from everyone whom she would tie that sacred thread. I was deeply agonized with such rubbish analysis.

I was never jealous of those boys of the lane towards whom sister Manju was affectionate. There was not even a single grievance in my mind for sister Manju. I was rather more cheerful that she had many brothers. If even Mani

Maa had considered anybody else as her son, I would not have developed the slightest narrow-mindedness towards her motherly affection. Rather many other sons would have availed the opportunity to bath in the Ganga of her motherly affection. I believe that the wealth of our love would have enriched more by that. Why should people like Mani Maa and sister Manju be imprisoned within the restricted territory of a particular family? Why should not they widen and expand the profuse warmth of their inner souls? If I have built family intimacy with anyone other than my family members, it is due to the impact and inspiration of the love of Mani Maa and sister Manju. They have taught me how to go beyond conditional relationships. They have also taught me how to love family members selflessly. It is doubtless that I have become rich with their warmth and intimacy but the question is how much of it have I been able to distribute among others?

Gradually I became a college professor and when Mani Maa came to know about it, her eyes sparkled more with pride. Whenever she found me, she used to drip my inner consciousness like an ever-flowing river in the same way as she used to bind me with her affectionate words when I was small. When I started addressing in different functions, she was found sitting among the audience to listen to me. When I spoke something emotionally on the stage, she was noticed to be ecstatic with overflowing emotions. She felt pride that her son was capable of delivering speeches standing on the stage. She would warn the nearby ladies to listen to her son silently.

When I started teaching in the college, many parents used to send marriage proposals to us through Mani Maa. My parents sought my opinion on those proposals. I could not make them understand my attitude towards marriage. It was suffocating for me to lead a stereotyped lifestyle. I was also thinking how upset Mani Maa would be with my disagreement. I did not want to marry and at the same time I did not want to make her unhappy. The entire day used to pass brooding over the matter. One afternoon Mani Maa herself approached me. She persuaded me in a tender voice to give my opinion. I felt she was ready to accept and consider my case if I expressed my thoughts freely before her. I ventilated my opinion before that idol of fortitude without any hesitation. She was not at all worried listening to me. Rather, she appreciated me telling, "O my son! How deep your experiences are! How lofty your thoughts are! Why should we obstruct your wishes?" She shared my opinion with my family members. She returned instilling great relief in my mind.

When Mani Maa came to our house intermittently, she would say, "Will you not invite your sister Manju in this Dussehra? She is eagerly waiting to meet you." She did not know what salary I was earning as a lecturer. She had an idea that all lecturers were paid equally. She would tell my parents, "Will you enjoy the salary of my son alone? Shall I not get a share?" My parents would reply, "Why not? Who can obstruct you to take your son's salary? Let him get a job in a government college, then you will have your share." It's very difficult to get a job in a government college.

One day Mani Maa requested me to purchase a saree for her. I suggested her to go to the nearby saree shop and select a saree of her choice. Mani Maa selected a costly saree. I honored her selection wholeheartedly. But my parents were a bit dissatisfied because of its high cost.

Finally the same saree was purchased as per Mani Maa's wish. My parents were worried. They were apprehensive of the difficulty in managing the house in case Mani Maa went on demanding things and forcing her son to spend money after her. If the entire salary of a month was devoted in purchasing a saree, how would the expenditure of the family be managed? I consoled my parents that if next time Mani Maa demanded any expensive thing, we would convey her our actual standard. I strongly believed that she would understand our condition and never put us in trouble.

After a few days we heard from a few relatives of our lane that Mani Maa expressed her utter satisfaction and likeness wearing that saree and told before everyone, "See, my son has purchased this saree for me." She felt like flying in the sky whenever she wore that saree. My eyes were filled with tears of elation when I heard about the mesmerizing reaction of Mani Maa. She wanted to convey everyone how worthy her son was and how he could purchase an expensive saree for his mother. She wished to spread the message among everyone in a loud voice that she had full right on her son and her son had intense love and respect for her. Being her son I could understand her approach very well.

After that I could not see Mani Maa for a long time. She stopped coming to our house. I requested my mother very often, "

If you see Mani Maa anywhere, tell her to come to our house." Unfortunately she did not turn up for months together.

After many days one early morning what I heard

about her from my mother, I cannot write here. Nobody can believe in such cruel words. Nobody can accept such a treachery. How could I?

She was so healthy and free of diseases. What happened to her immediately? Why were we not intimated? I heard that during her last stage she was admitted into the Government Hospital in front of our house. That night only her funeral rites were completed without intimating anything to anyone. Sister Manju went to her in law's house along with my elder father.

So many things happened without my knowledge. It was really afflicting that I could not see her affectionate face for once also in her last stage. Ruminating over this, I repented a lot and my heart was filled with awful suffering. I am her son. Wasn't it my duty to light her dead body on the pyre? Why was I not a part of her funeral rites? Normally I don't care for tradition. But I wanted to shed my hair to express the unbearable pain of separation from my mother. I remained in a deplorable state for days together whenever the incident flashed upon my mind.

I often sat by the window side of our upstairs and gazed at the hospital in the depth of the night. I communicated with Mani Maa, "Mother! Your last time passed near this house. Were you not interested even once to have a glance of your son? Did you not remember even once the tender face of your son? Today I am curious to call you "Maa" in the loudest voice. Why didn't you give me a chance to call like that in front of you Maa?"

I knew you would have never come to take my salary even if I had served in a government college. You told all those things for my happiness only, didn't you? Though nobody

else was able to understand your feelings, I knew your pious heart and soul. When you wanted to take something from me, you used to do that without the knowledge of anyone. When a smile blossomed on my face, your lap was showered with diamond pieces. The brightness of my eyes used to embellish your body with divine attire. How much have you been enthralled listening to my tottering words in my childhood? All those enthrallments had been attached to you like your invaluable ornaments. I don't know who else could see those divine resources in you, but I could see without any obscurity. I know very well why you demanded a saree that day. Why you were drenched with kindness. It was only to offer me an opportunity to do something for you. You wished to demonstrate before others your son's love and care for you, did not you?

Maa! Sometimes I think you were always overflowing with rapture. Didn't you remember me even once when you were sitting in seclusion? Didn't you think that a non-biological son could never be your own son how much love you might shower on him? Did you ever think that it would have been better if I had begotten from you? Were you not curious to keep me near you and claim all your rights as a mother? Whenever you found me, you sprayed happiness on me as if you could not feel the pain of separation. Perhaps you always felt the presence of your son inside your heart. You used to play, walk and talk with him and bequeath your motherly affection and rights on him. If it was not like that why you didn't tell for once, "O my son! If I had begotten you, you could have been fully my son, mine alone. I am helpless and unfulfilled not having you as my real son...."

Maa! How can I forget the bitter truth that I was not by your side during the last journey of your life? This reality is eating me from inside. My soul is crying bitterly. If you could really feel my presence near you, please emerge in my dream and reply-

"My Son! You always remained very close to me. When I was in the sickbed, it was you who was sitting near me. It was you who prayed God day and night to save my life. If you had not been with me, I must have called you. In my last stage I visualized only you, your tender face. You also gazed at me with tearful eyes addressing me as "Maa". You are still a baby for me. How innocent your face is! How transparent your eyes are! How sweet the word "Maa" sounds from your mouth! I heaved my last sigh hearing that sweet call. So why should I be upset?"

Maa! I am sorry I could not store your photo. I could not take a photo with you. How exhilarating you were while showing my saree to others! If I had stored your photograph, I could have told the world- 'See! This is my Mother.'

O my Mother! Do you know how much happy am I with my name Manindra? Please wipe out the guilt that I am not being identified with your name. Very often you emerge in my heart and say, "Your name is Manindra. You are the Indra of Mani. You are the pearl of Mani Maa. I am attached with your name. Wash the tears from your eyes, my dear son. I am always there with you."

Though I wish you to speak all these things in my dream, you are actually speaking in reality standing before me as a living image. Otherwise how could I think about all these things Maa? Your kind and nectarous face is always flashing before my eyes. How mirthful it is to observe that lustrous appearance! How peaceful it is! How soothing the sacred splashing of the light of love is! I am eternally melting from inside and outside with the celestial touch of that luminous light.

(Published in the Bishuba Issue of "Sabitri"-April, May, June 2014)

****

White Sugar

(1)

Why does the white face of White Sugar make me unsteady today? Do I know the mystery behind it?

Sometimes we feel as if we have forgotten our childhood friends but, in fact, they peep into our memory lane one after another like the stars in the evening sky. White Sugar was such a dazzling star. We were neither conscious nor capable to comprehend whose face was reflecting beauty in what way; we were just tied in a common thread of warmth. White Sugar was nobody else than my aunt. She was the apple of the eyes of the uncle and aunt of my middle elder mother. Her paper-white face was illuminated with the light of moon. May it be in a dark night or a moon-lit night, whenever I behold the white moon, my inner soul is overwhelmed with the memories of White Sugar.

The father of White Sugar had a grocery shop. Her parents and elder brothers used to sell various commodities sitting in the shop. Sometimes when the lane holding the grocery shop was deserted, the responsibility of the shop was conferred on White Sugar. As there was no crowd at that time, there was also no pressure on the seller. Occasionally some children would come to purchase chocolates. She would interact with the children so hilariously and be so much engrossed with them in merrymaking that any onlooker would think as though it was not a grocery shop but her most favourite play house.

The profound adoration and affection that my middle elder mother showered on me was matchless. When she went to her parental house or in other words, the house of my maternal uncle, at that time, I was an inseparable part of her saree-front. On the way her feet would spontaneously stop in front of the shop in which White Sugar was sitting. White Sugar would touch the heart of my elder mother with her affectionate call "Kaki". Those few moments of hearty interaction and exchange of emotion between my elder mother and White Sugar in standing position was so much fascinating that I think, people would fail to do the same so easily even in sitting position. The subject matter of their discussion was the worldly pain and pleasure. During the conversation, sometimes the eye of White Sugar dripped down the light of happiness and sometimes drops of tear like water drops dripping from the heart of the anguished clouds. No doubt, life is the store house of both pain and pleasure. I could feel the touch of both unconsciously as a little companion of my elder mother. During that unstoppable exchange of feelings White Sugar was physically present in front of us but psychologically wandering in a different world. She was looking like a fairy descended from the heaven. With her lovely, angelic smile she could drench and captivate the minds of her customers. White Sugar looked calm and serene as a clear string of river in a deserted path, as though she had no relation with the sufferings of this world. Like the rolling water on a lotus leave, her face emitted a heavenly aura that was the consequence of her successful victory in all sorts of tests related to human pain and pleasure.

After crossing the house of this uncle of my middle elder mother, we reached her eldest uncle's temple-like house. The intension was to enter that house and be engaged in the conversation with her eldest uncle for a prolonged time. I was a boy of hardly six or seven years. But, there was no inconsistency or volatility either in my body or mind. I used to sit very near to my elder mother for hours together with deep concentration. The eyes of the uncle of my elder mother (my grandfather) were illuminated with the rays of spiritual dedication. When her uncle was uttering words of wisdom and celestial things in a slow and soft voice sitting in a peaceful posture, the entire room was splattered with an ambience of tranquillity. After crossing that room when we moved ahead, we could see my grandmother, the aunt of my middle elder mother. She would appear before us with a fatigued, gloomy and withdrawn face reflecting profound afflictions, lamentations and adversities in both her eyes. She would be found with the remorseful, solemn and tearful plead of a dove.

After leaving the house of my grandparents when we were on our return journey, once again we used to meet White Sugar on the way. I have a lot of memory associated with her. Sometimes we were wandering and playing together in that narrow lane and sometimes inside the house of my grandparents: I am incapable of sketching all those memorable moments.

At the advent of evening, White Sugar would bid us farewell with a smile displaying her pearl-white teeth. After coming in contact with White Sugar one can feel how easy, beautiful and delightful life is. Amidst all sorts of family problems also her smile never lost its glitter. Even a full moon is once swallowed by the demon Rahu but the moonlight reflected from the face of White Sugar was incessantly scattering a cool aura in all circumstances.

When I was taking the Annual Examination of Std. III, at that time we were shifted to our new house from the old one. Though I was intermittently going through the lane of White Sugar with my middle elder mother, but gradually it slowed down. As I grew up, the frequency decreased accordingly.

After completing primary education, I was enrolled into high school. By the time I entered into Std. VIII & IX, I lost enthusiasm towards games and sports that was inculcated in me till Std. VII. After that, for many days together, may be for years, I did not go towards the house of White Sugar with my elder mother.

(2)

After a long interval when once again I got an opportunity to see White Sugar, I was amazed to see that she was no more that smiling and humorous White Sugar of the past. Her entire face was enveloped with a layer of gloominess as the dark cloud-covered-moon producing an unpleasant tune. I could not understand the reason behind that drastic transformation. In her family she was the only gifted girl among her three brothers. All the family members and the people of neighbourhood loved her warmly. In spite of being surrounded with such warmth and intimacy why her white lotus face had lost its glaze, I was unable to understand. Though her face was supposed to be glittered more prominently with the beauty and charm of her youth, why there was reflection of overshadowing pain and suffering, I had no idea about that. When I was passing silently through that lane, I just took a cursory glance of her grieving face. The grocery shop had been established perhaps before the birth of White Sugar. When she took her birth, her fair complexion had a resemblance with the white sugar which was being unloaded in the shop in gunny sacks. I think, for that reason she was named as "Dhob Chini" in Sambalpuri language which means white sugar in English. Not only her face was as white but also her voice was as sweet as sugar. In this way she could justify her name every moment.

I think it happened before I was reading in college. During one of my visits to our old house, I was moving towards the main road through the lane of White Sugar very cautiously. While crossing that most familiar narrow lane, I was quite alert not to be either noticed or called by any of the members of my maternal uncle's house. I found White Sugar sitting in the shop in the same way as she used to sit before ten years. On the demand of a particular commodity by a customer, she just stood up turning her back towards the road in order to fetch it from a nearby wooden shelf. I was startled to notice her back side then. What I saw was unbelievable. I was in doubt whether that was the back side of White Sugar or a mound. Carrying the burden of that mound which is also called hunchback, White Sugar was standing there. Within no time the secrete behind her sadness was revealed to me. Because of her hunch she could not be nominated as a suitable match for any bridegroom. Her evil destiny had drawn a full stop to all the sweet dreams of her marriage.

How sad! White Sugar must have been thrilled with thousands of aspirations to form a small family of her own. She must have constantly dreamt of her imaginary hero, her life partner. But this hunch stood up as an obstacle devastating all her sweet dreams and discolouring her fine and delicate sentiments. Was the back of White Sugar the only suitable place for the hunch to expand itself? Instead of searching for any other place, that fleshy lump started increasing its height day by day on the back of White Sugar. My eyes were deliberately moist with unrestrained tears. I could not summon up courage to see her face. So I moved ahead towards our house. I was reluctant to share my sorrowful feelings, my miseries of being speechless with anyone, not even with my middle elder mother.

After that I passed through the shop of White Sugar many a times. I could see her closely from her front and

back. Once the advent of this unwanted hunch and the subsequent gloominess on her face had made me startled. However, later on also, I was startled repeatedly because her face had revived the previous glow and glaze. The dark cloud of despair could no more envelope her face. The way she used to display a pure and innocent smile in the past, she started continuing the same then also. Surprisingly, she was found talking with everyone very cheerfully with glances of simplicity and beauty. I had a wrong notion that all the dreams, ambitions, desires and happiness of White Sugar had been devastated by the hunch on her back. However, the fact was that it was she herself who had destroyed all her misfortunes, afflictions, worries and apprehensions with her bold determination. No doubt, the toad-like hunch was heavily sitting on her back swallowing her happiness and releasing unspeakable pain for her. But, the triumphant glaze of her face could drive out that pain from her mind for ever. Her tenacious decision to accept the bitter truth of her life with ease and smile had gifted her with a divine beauty. She knew that she was not the humpbacked maid of Kansa who would be liberated from the curse with the divine touch of Lord Sri Krishna, but she was mentally liberated from the humpback as she had deeply felt the eternal existence of Sri Krishna in her heart. Moreover, I felt that she had developed a likeness towards that dangling hunch as though it was her pampered child. She had perhaps considered the hunch as her most affectionate little son.

(3)

Many years have elapsed since I have seen her. As told earlier, she is my aunt, just similar to my mother. When I recollect her memories, I feel, I am recollecting the memories of another adoring mother. It is true. My heart is being accomplished with the touch of new affection when I virtually address her as "Maa". The way she looked at me, smiled at me and came closer to me from my childhood days, simply displayed her unconditional motherly love towards me. At present my middle elder mother is no more in this world. The parents of White Sugar are also no more. But White Sugar still exists with her brother and sister-in-law along with their children. She is endowed with such paramount patience, stability, calmness and confidence of a female ascetic that her hunch can never maintain the same.

At present I don't call White Sugar by her name. The line which my heart utters repeatedly vibrating my whole body is – "White Sugar is a mother for me".

Published in the 8th issue of "Jhankar"-November 2022

****

About a Suicide

Once I had to stay in the hostel during Christmas holidays. I was a student of post graduation then. I am narrating an incident of that time.

I had come home before two/three days of the vacation as I had to remain in the hostel the entire vacation. I reached the hostel on the very first day of the vacation. I was expected to remain in the hostel for the printing work of our literary magazine.

As soon as I reached the campus, I was startled with what I heard from other students. One hosteller committed suicide last night. The dead body of the student had already been cremated after post mortem. His funeral rites were executed by the students of that hostel only as his parents did not turn up even after being informed.

Most of the students left the hostel and went to their respective homes during the Christmas carrying the pathos of such a horrible incident. But I had to stay in the hostel. I was puzzled thinking about the boy who had committed suicide and his parents. I was unable to understand anything. I did not know the boy also as he was not someone from our department. Moreover, I had joined the hostel as a new- comer. I knew only a few students there.

Some of my friends tried to draw an outline of the boy in my mind by narrating his physical features. But I was unable to recall the face of that student. However, I pretended that I was able to recollect the face of that boy.

A few of my classmates were still there in the hostel. That night we had an elaborate discussion on that boy which continued till midnight. We were unable to know the reason behind that suicidal attempt. But some of my classmates anticipated that the boy did so being unable to tolerate the cruelties of his parents. It

was really mysterious and surprising that neither his parents nor his acquaintances came to collect his corpse.

The name of that boy was Vijay. The local police informed that Vijay had written a letter before his death. In that letter it was confessed that no one was responsible for Vijay's death. Some of the lines of that letter in the language of my classmates were- "I love this beautiful winter evening so much. The sights of many such winter evenings are flashing upon my inward eyes. I am looking at these twinkling stars through my windows. I don't want to die today."

I was also overwhelmed listening to these lines. How beautiful indeed human life is! In spite of the thousand cruelties of others, man wants to live in this world for the splendor of the infinite blue sky, the green trees, the multi-colored flowers and the chattering of birds. Vijay had better postpone his plan at least for that day! He had better realize the importance of his gifted life! If he thought to commit suicide for the cruelties of human beings, he could have thought of living at least for those dazzling stars and the cheerful evenings! Those stars and wintry evenings were motivating him to remain alive in this fascinating world. How he couldn't understand that!

That night seemed to be very quiet and solemn in the hostel. Every corner was enveloped with the shadow of lamentation. When I was sleeping alone in my hostel room at night, I was repeatedly thinking- "How can I spend my entire vacation alone here ? How deserted and weird the atmosphere has become!"

When I woke up in the morning, I found my remaining friends getting ready to leave the hostel for home. The hostel was going to be completely empty after their departure. I asked myself, "Shall I live alone in this three-storey building with more than hundred rooms? Shall I experience alone every moment the horrible situation spread everywhere?"

At the time of departure my classmates warned me once more to be careful. I felt a heavy burden in my heart. All left me alone to face the terrible situation. I was thinking that it would be better if anyone had been there to accompany me- no matter if unknown to me also.

It was late night when I returned from the press after the proof reading of our literary magazine. The entire hostel was filled in darkness. My heart was beating faster in that darkness. Still I summoned up courage and moved towards my room. Once reached, it was not possible to come back from my room. I spat gurgling my throat loudly. I unlocked the room and switched on the light. My room was illuminated. Then I moved towards the bath room. The bathroom side was completely dark. Perhaps the bulbs had been stolen by someone. I washed my face, hands and feet in the darkness producing a loud sound. When I came back, I trembled with nervousness. There was no light in my room. I stood speechless. I could not understand what happened to the light. Did anyone enter my room? Did anyone extinguish the bulb? Countless questions arose in my mind. Feeling helpless I slowly entered the room, took out a candle and a matchbox from the drawer and lighted the candle. With the help of the candle light I tried to find out what was wrong inside the room but felt somehow relieved to find everything normal. Actually the bulb had been fused. I shut the front door and locked it from inside. My heart was pounding faster. I had never experienced such an awful situation especially after an unexpected incident of suicide.

I recalled repeatedly the facts related to the desperate attempt of Vijay. He tied a thick rope around his neck and attempted to hang from the fan. When Vijay's friends did not get any response after a prolonged knocking on his door, the matter was informed to the police. The police had to break the railings of the backside window to open the door. After opening the door, everybody was thunder-struck to find the dead body of Vijay hanging from the fan.

Vijay's memory accelerated the sensation of emptiness in my heart. I opened my window and threw a cursory glance at all the rooms upstairs expecting the presence of any one in any room. Suddenly, a ray of hope made my pounding heart slightly relaxed. In the left side of the upper floor I found the reflection of the light of a room coming through the sky light. I presumed that a certain student must have decided to stay back in hostel to execute some important tasks in that vacation. I felt abundant solace when I thought that a fellow companion was there with me in the hostel during the vacation and I did not have to stay in that terrific surrounding alone. In fact, this was for the first time that the hostel had been empty during a vacation. Even in the long summer vacations of yesteryears, the hostel was found packed with students who used to prepare for various examinations. But that year the situation was somehow different. Nevertheless, the presence of someone upstairs was a great relief to my solitude. I thought to visit that room and meet that student once. It would be a blessing if the student came out to be either my classmate or any known person. I locked my room and moved towards the other room. I had to climb the steps in utter darkness. Suddenly a different thought crept into my mind- perhaps the residents of that room might have forgotten to switch off the bulbs in a hurry. This idea puzzled the certainty of getting a companion in that room. Anyways, I reached that room with a variety of contrasting thoughts. I was glad to see that the room was not locked from outside. That certified the presence of someone inside.

I thumped on the door.

Somebody opened the door after one minute. It was a student who was unknown to me. He looked at me in questioning eyes. His book was open on his table. It gave me the notion that he was reading the book before my arrival. I could not understand how to start a conversation with him. I just asked politely, "Have I disturbed you?" The student replied in negative and asked me what my purpose was. I thought to tell him the truth only.

I said, "No, no, nothing significant. The hostel has been completely empty and I am living alone downstairs. The light of your room infused in me the hope of getting a fellow companion in this empty hostel."

The student said, "It's my great pleasure. Please come in and have a seat."

I went inside and sat in the bed. He sat in a chair. He seemed to be a student from senior class. It was certain that he belonged to the same hostel and was also staying near me. I thought it would be considered my weakness if I projected that I was not acquainted with him before. Thus, I didn't ask him anything. He also didn't ask me anything. Our only recognition was that we both belonged to the same hostel block and that was enough at that time.

The student seemed very meek and mild. He was looking at me. I was not able to decide what to speak. Moreover, discussing anything other than Vijay's topic would seem very absurd at that time. But the truth was that I was least interested to open that topic.

Nevertheless, I had to break the silence first— "Oh my God! What a shocking incident happened!"

"Yes, this is what life is", he answered briefly.

He was not a gossip-lover, nor was I. So we could not communicate much with each other.

I took farewell from him after exchanging a few words on some general topics like the then prevailing darkness in the hostel, the bulbs being stolen, insufficient water in the tank on usual days as compared to the large no of students and availability of enough water for the use of both of us during the vacation etc.

I had a sound sleep that night.

During those days I used to go to the press for proof-reading after12.00 'O' clock taking my bath. After proof-reading, I used to wander here and there for some time and then return to my hostel room at night. I was not in any tension as I had a fellow companion there. Occasionally I used to visit him and after exchanging a few words of wellbeing, come back to my room. My room was also well-lit then with a new bulb. There was absolutely no problem at all. But I was lacking courage to discuss about Vijay with that boy at night. One afternoon I summoned up courage and asked the boy about Vijay during my visit to his room- "Well, do you know why Vijay committed suicide actually?"

He was silent for some time and then told, "When a man doesn't get a real well-wisher, a true friend, a near and dear one in his life, he loses all interest of survival."

That day afternoon the sky was looking more vibrant in deep blue color. The wintry sun-light was so soothing. I was looking outside through the window. Being unable to conceal my feelings I said, "See, how beautiful the sky is! The birds are singing their melodious songs from the other side. How can someone attempt to die leaving this fascinating world? I can't imagine it also."

He said, "It's not true that after suicide one can leave this world and proceed to another world. It's not so easy to go to another world as per one's desire. Even after death one remains in this world only. The way one used to be enchanted with the beautiful things of this world during one's life, after death also one can be enchanted in the same way".

I was glad to hear his answer. He went on speaking as though he was a student of Philosophy. I told, "Alright, but I have heard that the spirit of a suicidal victim wanders all around because of his unfulfilled desires."

"Yes, certainly. After death he realizes that he is still not free from the pain of unfulfilled desires, the anguish of unpleasantness for which he had committed suicide and from which he wanted freedom. Suicide can never be the solution of any problem."

I was listening to his words with rapt attention. It was time for me to go to the press. When I took a leave from him, he told again, "What a man knows after his death, he wants to convey the same to those who are alive. He wants to tell that his soul has not been emancipated yet. He is still burning in the same agony even after his death. In fact, his agony has increased more."

I proceeded to the press overwhelmed with his words. Gradually as my workload increased, I could not get enough time to meet my sole companion of the hostel. On the other hand, I could not feel loneliness due to my busy schedule. I remained fully engaged in my work only.

The university reopened on 2nd of January. All students came back to the hostel. The deserted hostel was again filled with the shouts and cheers of the students. I was also relieved after spending my vacation smoothly. All my classmates came back. Anand asked, "Pradyot, were you alone in the hostel during the vacation?"

I replied confusingly, "Yes brother, I was almost alone. Of course, I chanced to be associated with a companion here."

Other students also came to know about my stay in the hostel alone. My press work was over and regular classes resumed.

After a few days......

One Sunday afternoon I went to Sarat's room for a gossip. He was my classmate. During our conversation again we opened the topic of Vijay's suicide. It was not easy on the part of anyone to forget that incident. Sarat went on talking about Vijay endlessly. He asked me, "Have you seen him, Pradyot?"

"I must have seen him but not able to recall his face exactly", I replied hesitatingly.

"Strange! Everyone is familiar with him except you".

After telling so Sarat took out a photo album from his cupboard. "Luckily I have kept his photo safe in this album. I had collected it from him a few days before his attempt.... but... what for shall I see this photo when he is no more?", gripped with emotion Sarat showed me Vijay's photo turning over the pages of the album.

After I saw the photograph, I stood absolutely stunned and speechless. I felt as if there was no soil under my feet. It was unbelievable! He was the same fellow with whom I had discussed so many things during the vacation. It was only for him that I could stay in the hostel without any trouble.

I said strongly, "No no! This boy can never be Vijay. I have talked with this boy several times during the vacation. In fact, because of this boy only I was able to spend the holidays fearlessly."

I narrated everything to Sarat.

He was surprised and considered it unbelievable. He also knew my nature and believed that I was speaking the truth only.

I said, "Let's go to that room and I'll prove the presence of this boy there."

Of course, after vacation I had not seen that boy again. Anyways, as per planning we both went to that room where I had conversed many times with him.

Sarat pointed at the room and said, "This is the room in which he committed suicide. The police had to unlock the door by breaking the railings of the backside window.

From here only his dead body was rescued. The room is still in its former condition. Nobody has locked it also. After the rescue of the dead body the police collected only Vijay's diary, a few note books and his letters.

I analyzed and reviewed the whole incident. It was after my return from home that I came to know about Vijay's suicide but I never tried to know in which room he was staying. I didn't feel the necessity of asking anyone either. I was shocked when I realized that I was talking with the spirit a dead person in that room all those days.

I was still not in a position to accept that Vijay was not present in his room.

I terribly wanted to surprise Sarat and others by discovering Vijay in that room. I was unable to forget those cherished conversations I had made with Vijay. His face was still flashing in my memory lane. Each and every word spoken by him was still ringing around my ears.

I thought to amaze everyone by giving evidences of the existence of Vijay. Then I suddenly pushed the door of that room.

(Published in Budharaja-1992)

****

Welcome to Sharada

Ramakrishna Paramahamsa stood stunned for a few moments listening to the proposal. He had never imagined before that he would have to face such a problematic situation so abruptly. Then what was his obligation at that moment? How should he confront with that unsolicitated difficulty?

Sometimes he forgot about the proposal spontaneously. But when again it came back to his memory, he became extremely worried. When he woke up from half sleep at midnight, his mind was perplexed and overburdened with the same thoughts. Then he uttered only one word- 'Maa', 'Maa', 'Maa'. During his complete absorption in the thoughts of Maa Kali when deep sleep usually embraced him, he had no idea of it. However, when he got up in the morning, the same thoughts came back to disturb and trouble his mind again for a long period of time.

At last, he could clearly see the way to tackle the problem. He asked himself, "O my crazy mind! How couldn't you find the way which was the easiest one?" After that he proceeded ahead and entered into the temple of Goddess Dakshineswar Kali as he did every day. He could behold his loving 'Maa' manifested in the form of a vivacious idol. Ramakrishna never saw Goddess Kali's furious face with her flowing red tongue, sparkling wide eyes and her neck encircled with a garland of skulls. In fact, when he took a glance of the face of Maa Kali, her terrible face used to turn into a calm and peaceful face, full of love and affection for her children. Ah! That serene and affectionate appearance, that profound motherly warmth and adoration captivated his total attention. Everyday Ramakrishna was thrilled and mesmerized beholding the affectionate face of Goddess Kali. While it was quite impossible on the part of others to have such a serene vision of Goddess Kali, Ramakrishna was constantly absorbed in the vision of that benign, poignant and blissful Maa and having absolute peace and tranquility in his heart and soul. When he offered her Prasad, he wept like a small child and pleaded her to accept it. At that time the Divine Mother descended from her shrine and emerged before him as a living human being. Moreover, she would carry Ramakrishna in her divine lap and with an ever-smiling face she would feed him the celestial Prasad. Ramakrishna would also feed the leftover Prasad to his Maa in tearful eyes. All these events might seem absurd or impossible for somebody else but for Ramakrishna those were the naked truth of his life. At night he invited Maa and like an infant he slept peacefully embellishing the lap of the Divine Mother. He was virtually on a never-ceasing divine communication with her. He could not share such kind of spiritual experience with anyone. But gradually, the truth of his deep inclination towards the Goddess came to the knowledge of everyone. Earlier there was no such devoted priest in that temple. So the news of Ramakrishna's spiritually absorbed mind and unusual behavior reached to Kamarpukur. When his family members knew about the matter, they were intensely worried. They firmly decided to bring Ramakrishna back to normal condition.

Ramakrishna's family members decided to get him married. They thought that after marriage Ramakrishna would be bound to accept responsibility and keep his attention on normal affairs rather than his spiritual practices and vision. In that way, marriage would be a good steadying influence upon him. It was the marriage proposal of his family members that had troubled Ramakrishna that day. Being unable to take a resolution and find any other alternative way, Ramakrishna proceeded to the temple, stood in front of his ever-venerated Maa Kali. He washed her feet with his incessant tears. Then he kept his palms on her lotus-feet, bowed his head on the ground and wept loudly telling, "O my Mother! Kindly usher your divine blessings on me, remove my problems and release me from this hard time instantly. Except you there is nobody in this world who can understand me." He went on crying for hours together oblivion to himself. Soon after this a clear voice could be heard. It told softly, "Ramakrishna! First you get up and listen to me." It was not a new voice. Ramakrishna was well acquainted with this affectionate voice. He was often overwhelmed listening to this sweet voice of the Divine Mother. As the sweet notes of Srikrishna's flute carries Sriradha to the cavity of forgetfulness, the sweetness in the voice of the Divine Mother dragged Ramakrishna to a different world. The subtle tune of the Veena of Maa Saraswati, the Goddess of Speech, jingled from this voice. Moreover, one could hear exceptional musical notes from it. It was in this voice that Ramakrishna received the magnanimity of the offerings of Mahalaxmi, the Goddess of luxury. Now Ramakrishna lifted his head and beheld his most familiar, most intimate image of Maa Kali. When he was wrapped up with the overwhelming influence of Maa Kali, he noticed that inside the image of Maa Kali there was the reflection of another calm and charming image with the face of a lotus. It was a deserted night and what kind of silent communication occurred between Ramakrishna and Maa Kali that night, nobody had the slightest notion of it. Next day, Ramakrishna sent a message to Kamarpukur that he was ready to act as per the wish of his family members. He further informed his family members that there was no need of wasting time by visiting to so many houses. They needed to go straight to the house of Ramachandra Mukherjee in Jayrambati to find the bride.

The family members were startled at Ramakrishna's message. They were relieved too. Without making any further delay they proceeded to Jayrambati. After reaching there, they wanted to see the affectionate daughter of Ramachandra Mukherjee. Immediately a five-year-old girl, Saradamani came and adorned the knees of Ramakrishna's mother. The family members were startled and speechless. They were bewildered thinking how could that five-year-old girl be the life partner of twenty three-year-old Ramakrishna? They could not easily accept the huge age difference between the bride and the bridegroom. But then they also gave a serious thought to Ramakrishna's own proposal to go straight to that house and choose that particular girl. They were quite apprehensive that if Ramakrishna did not marry the girl of his choice, he might be disturbed and never give his consent for marriage again. Finally, Ramakrishna's family members agreed in the proposal. Initially it was difficult even for Ramachandra Mukherjee to take a decision. However, after gathering knowledge on Ramakrishna's character and personality and ensuring his daughter's safe future, he also consented for the marriage.

That most awaited moment reached very soon. The date of marriage was fixed. The crazy Ramakrishna was decorated as the bridegroom. The bridegroom's party proceeded towards Jayrambati. As customary in those days, the bride's face was usually covered with a long veil. Therefore, the bridegroom could not get an opportunity to see it. However, the situation of Saradamani was different. At the age of five she was completely devoid of any sort of coyness and hesitation. She was found running from one side of the house to the other and engaged in playful activities. When Saradamani was brought to the marriage platform, accidentally her eyes met with the eyes of Ramakrishna. Remembering his rare emotional exchange with the Divine Mother that night, Ramakrishna took just a small glance of Saradamani. Then his lips were adorned with a bright smile. On his face blossomed at once thousand buds of tuberoses. Saradamani was too young to understand anything. But she felt that her bridegroom was her most cherished and recognizable person.

In this way the marriage was duly solemnized. The family members felt relaxed thinking that after marriage Ramakrishna would stop behaving unusually and shoulder family responsibility gradually. Sharada had to remain in Jayrambati till she attended her youth. At the age of 18, she came to her in-law's house. She had to spend her days and nights in endless waiting for Ramakrishna. But, Ramakrishna never turned up. She came to know that Ramakrishna was demonstrating more unusual and unexpected behavior like a mad man those days. At last she was instructed to go near Ramakrishna. Sharada was in a dilemma how to meet her crazy husband. Anyways, she gathered courage and was mentally ready to go to Dakshineswar Kali temple. She crossed the entire distance on her foot. Finally, when she reached the temple gate, she found Ramakrishna coming out of the temple after worshipping Maa Kali. Now it was time for the distribution of Prasad. Being completely exhausted with toil and sweat when Sharada entered the temple, she was astounded with the touch of a bright light that resembled the flashing of a lightening.

Ramakrishna received good news of the arrival of Sharada. He was relieved and said, "So, you came here finally." He rushed to Maa Sharada as a child rushes to its loving mother. Ramakrishna gazed at the eyes of Sharada and noticed the same image of his affectionate Maa Kali mirrored on her face. That night when he took a final decision of his marriage, he had seen the mirroring of Sharada's face on the face of Maa Kali. He ensured that it was his Divine Mother only who had descended to his life in human figure. The Divine Mother had promised him that night – "Why are you worried Ramakrishna? I'll come to your life in a human incarnation, not as your wife but as your mother." That single line uttered from the lips of Maa Kali echoed in the heart of Ramakrishna. He realized at once that the Divine Mother had taken human embodiment in the name of Sharada to look after him and shower on him her profuse love and affection. No more doubts remained in him.

Ramakrishna recalled the vision of the calm and peaceful face of the Mother with a beautiful smile that he had experienced alone that night. He found the same reflection in the eyes and face of Sharada. Then his heart was surcharged with deep emotion for Sharada. He came closer to her and said in a shivering voice, "You have come to me Maa. So nice of you. I was waiting for your auspicious

emersion from many years." Sharada could not believe that
Ramakrishna had accepted her so naturally and easily. The
lustrous sparkle of light, which was ignited from the face of
Ramakrishna, came quickly and penetrated into her heart.
After that, her heart-beats grew faster and she realized that
Ramakrishna was her most intimate and known person,
very near to her heart. The eyes of both Ramakrishna and
Sharada were splattered with tears of enchantment. Sharada
went on thinking, "Who is Ramakrishna? What kind of
relationship have I with him? Is he my husband? Is he
nothing else than my husband?" In her eyes Ramakrishna
did not seem to be a man glittering with the aura of youth,
rather he seemed like a child full of innocence. She wished
to carry that seemingly familiar head of Ramakrishna in her
lap and kiss on it with her shivering lips moist with tender
motherly fondness. She was no more the earlier Sharada.
The moment she stepped into Dakshineswar Kali Temple,
she had turned into an altogether different personality.

The radiant light of lightening entered into her heart and soul, had changed all her feelings and outlook towards Ramakrishna at once. Her inner spirit was initially troubled with the apprehension of whether she would be accepted by Ramakrishna or not. But, at that very moment, it was enveloped with extreme peace and contentment. She could hear the heart-touching divine tune from all directions of the temple. In that tune was jingling the pious chants of welcome to Sharada.

Sharada was gazing at the face of Ramakrishna without an inkling of her eyes. Ramakrishna was taking her to the Mother of the World with eyes of gratitude and tears.

(Published in the issue of October 2019 of "Srujana Swapna")

****

Let me be Defamed for Shyama

From my childhood days I was overwhelmed to see Him in His portrait hanging from the wall. What an enchanting, smooth and serene appearance He has! How mesmerizing are His curling locks of hair covering His forehead! The dense, curly and black hair on His head looks marvelous. His hands are adorned with a flute made up of a small piece of bamboo. The edges of His two beautiful eyes are embellished with two narrow lines of collyrium. His handsome head is splendidly decorated with a colorful peacock feather. Words fall short to describe His electrifying beauty and magnanimity. I am unable to describe His nectarous handsomeness any more as I am not fortunate enough to be as glorious and talented as Abhimanyu Samanta Singhara or Bhakta Charan or Sri Gopalakrushna or Dinakrushna.

When I was a child it was my middle elder mother who had intensely enlivened the image of Lord Sri Krishna in my heart. Her lips always uttered the divine tales of Lord Sri Krishna. Each and every word that she uttered enthrallingly in appreciation of Sri Krishna eventually changed my perception towards Him and turned His portrait into a living image. I had no idea that the enchanting picture of Sri Krishna had already enveloped the sky of my mind with a deep inclination towards Him.

In those days a number of dramas were being staged near our residence. Once the artists of Arnapurna Theater enacted around 30 plays for one month. One of those plays named 'Manabhanjan' is still fresh in my memory. That play had been enacted on the 29th night and I was an ardent and engrossed spectator of that night. I can never forget the divine experience of that night throughout my life.

During the winter season also many drama groups used to come to our locality to enact a variety of dramas for months together. Even today, my heart is enchanted with the memory of that midnight play in which I had seen the living image of my favorite Lord Sri Krishna. It was beyond my imagination how a small boy of my age playing the role of Sri Krishna drove me away to Gopapura in a single night with his poignant acting. What an aura of blue light was sprouting from the two blue lotus eyes of that little Krishna! How animated, lustrous and heart-piercing were the glances and playful movements of his dark eyes! My engrossed mind used to lose itself in those eyes that had the depth and infinity of the blue sky. I used to pray endlessly for his sweetest glances to fall on me at least once for a fraction of moment. How eager I was to amalgamate my eyes with his deep blue sea-like eyes at least for a second! At the same time I knew that he had descended onto the stage to spread his warm and affectionate glances on everyone. So why should his graceful attention be centered on me in particular without any reason?

Anyways, the play came to an end at the end of the night but my heart started singing an evening song of excitement. That song was enveloped with the sweet notes of the flute. For a few days my mind was travelling in the creeper groves of Gopapura. I was not in a naturally conscious state. The

sweet glances and charismatic movements of those blue eyes made me spell bound each moment.

Every moment I was searching for that boy of my age.-my little Krishna. One Sunday afternoon when I was heading towards the guest house of our locality, I saw my little Krishna stepping forward with his amazing and hypnotic gesture. He was accompanied by one of his chums. Honey-sweet words were dripping from his glossy and pink lips. Of course, I could not hear those sweet words from a distance though I had kept my ears quite alert. However, I could smell the fragrance of his loving words which were anointed with many flowers of aromatic scents. My inner voice prompted me to stop a while. My heart wanted me to pull him near me. But I was lacking courage to initiate any such daring attempt. Today, after reading the poem of Gopalakrushna, my heart sings, "I wish to see you every time farther or nearer." For a few days I was waiting for his arrival and departure through that dusty road attached to the guest house. The road seemed to be the sandy, brown road of Gopapura and for me it had become a path of pilgrimage. I was waiting for hours together looking in and out of the guest house for my cherished little Krishna to appear. I knew that he might not see me but the thirst of my eyes would be certainly quenched with a single vision of his striking face even from a distance. I was peeping at him through secret places so that he would be unknown to my deeds. Undoubtedly, he was looking stunning and highly fascinating with fine make up and gorgeous attire on the lavishly decorated stage with incandescent lights at night. But even during day time without make up and gorgeous attire also he was looking indescribably enchanting. His two small, simple and innocent eyes were overflowing with the ripples of a variety of emotions. When he was talking with his friend softly, his lips emitted the fragrance of thousand lotus petals. How captivating the bunches of his curly hair were! I was really lacking knowledge and capability that day and even today to estimate whether that boy had been chosen by the officials of the drama committee to play the role of Sri Krishna or Lord Sri Krishna Himself had descended onto the earth carrying the nature and form of that little boy.

Every day evening came followed by the night but that particular drama was never enacted once again. Nevertheless, I wanted to see him the whole night till my heart's content whatever role he might be playing in whichever drama. That is why I was booking tickets every night to discover him in new incarnations. Every night he used to mesmerize and delight me when he mounted the stage irrespective of which day it was and what role he was playing. I was praying incessantly, "O' Shyama! May your kind eyes fall on me only once. That will make my life really pious and blissful." An innocent boy like me did not know whether my silent message could reach him or not. I was too shy to open my mouth and too ignorant of expressing my feelings. In fact, I followed my little Krishna for months together but could not gather courage to utter a single word for him. In spite of that somewhere in a corner of my heart I had a belief that I would be able to exchange my feelings with him some day. I would be able to invite him to our house and make him sit directly in front of my loving elder mother. There was no reason for my wish to wither away but unfortunately, one day when I returned from school, I mounted our concrete terrace and was utterly shocked to see that the drama ground was looking deserted. All the paraphernalia of the drama troops were being loaded in a number of trucks. The huge emptiness prevailing in each and every corner of the ground clearly indicated that the actors and actresses had already left the place earlier. My eyes were covered with tears. Then they started rolling down without any stoppage. All my wishes and prayers were swept away in the tsunami of my tears. My heart was overburdened with disappointments and complaints. I stood in front of the portrait of Shyama and said, "Is it fair?"

I am still unknown what I was for Him-whether one of his Gopal friends or His beloved Sri Radha or the affectionate mother Yashoda or His great devotee Kubja who was eagerly waiting for Him in Mathura. Though I didn't know what I was for Him, but He is omniscient to understand my feelings. That is why remaining awake for many nights I repeatedly asked him in a gasping voice and tearful eyes, "Why did you play with my emotion?"

****

Father:- An Endless Treatise of Life

There is not a single moment in my life when the image of my father has not emerged in my memory. Nevertheless, today, after reading Rabindranath Tagore's "Khokababur Pratyabartan", I cannot restrain my tears; I cannot control my overflowing emotions.

My father was an ordinary employee in the Sambalpuri Handloom Boutique. He was skilled in managing his family with his petty salary which I could realize later on when I grew up. There was not a single minute when I could experience the poverty of my father or my family either in my infancy or in childhood or even in my youth. Whatever I wished, it was readily available for me. All my demands, wishes and requests used to be sanctioned by my father without a fraction of delay. For that reason my father was often laughed at and satirized by his co-workers and friends. The members inside and outside his family used to mock at him for molly-coddling me. But, he did not care for that. He was determined to nurture me with the best provisions. I am utterly amazed thinking about that.

According to my father, when the American Friends Society started working at Barpali, he joined it as a translator. When he saw an American doctor cleaning the flesh wounds of the lepers without contempt, a drastic change occurred in his outlook. During my childhood when I was falling down and having injuries on many parts of my body, he used to clean the suppurated wounds regularly with so much of love and care. When I remember those incidents now, my heart is pounded profusely with sorrow. My father was so big-hearted not only towards me but also towards other family members. He did not hesitate to cleanse even the excreta of his father and elder brother.

I am startled to realize how magnanimous fathers are! It was my father who used to shop all my garments till I became a lecturer. It was he who used to take me to the doctor when I was unwell. At times when I was reluctant to go to the doctor, he used to consult the doctor himself and bring medicine for me even at midnight. Alas! In return to all his benevolent services, I have done nothing for him. When both of his kidneys got damaged, he was very often being taken to the hospital for treatment. Very often his body was supplied with blood. During his treatment, whosoever was paying a visit to him, he used to admire me profoundly in front of the visitor. In fact, the person who had completely devoted herself in the service of father was my mother, not me.

Today, that story of Rabindranath is repeatedly ringing in my mind. In that story when a servant named Raicharan was playing with Khoka Babu, the son of Anukul Babu, his Zamindar master, on the bank of river Padma, at that time he lost the child due to his little negligence. The swelling waves of the river swept away the toddler in a fraction of moment when Raicharan himself was plucking flowers on a Kadam tree to fulfill the toddler's demand. When Raicharan did not find the toddler, he screamed out of the depths of his broken heart. He was not in a position to share his master this inconsolable news of irreparable loss. Through his screams he just tried to convey that he did not know anything. The toddler was engulfed by river Padma. The candle of his life extinguished forever. But the wife of Anukul Babu thought that Raicharan had taken her child away for the sake of the gold and silver ornaments he had on. The heart of Raicharan broke down into pieces. At his adulthood he was driven out of the house of his master. But the crux of the matter was that Raicharan was issueless by that time. Just after one year of that event he was blessed with a baby boy. The child mesmerized Raicharan with his conversational style, body language and surging feelings in his eyes. He was surprised to discover in his own son the same appearance, attributes, gesture and posture which Khoka Babu was having. Though Raicharan was in utter poverty but he started nurturing his son by providing all luxuries and care that the child of an aristocratic family generally avails.

My father was nurturing me just like that since my infancy. I always felt myself to be the son of a royal family. My books, copies, pen, outfits –everything was distinguished with the sign of aristocracy. I never faced any sort of scarcity in my life.

My father's contributions do not end here. When I recall what else he was doing for me, I find my heart breaking into pieces. He used to clean and polish my shoes till he was alive. If he went to toilet and during that time I needed to use the same, he would vacate the toilet for me immediately after hearing mother's knock on the door. He used to talk with me with so much of courtesy and graciousness that I felt somehow uncomfortable. If I was found standing while discussing something with him, he would not allow me to stand even for a minute. As we request our guest to adorn the most honored chair, in the same way he would request me to sit down. Sometimes I was amazed with such behavior of father. I did not understand what was the need of such courtesy, such cultured and polite behavior? Was I a guest? Was I not his own son? Sometimes it also crept into my mind that perhaps I was an outsider who had come to that family as a guest. I have always received high standard treatment from him. He would always store delicious food for me. He was a great devotee of his own father. When his father was alive, my father could not purchase a fan for him due to poverty. But when he died even if my father was able to purchase a fan, he deprived himself from the comfort of fan as a repentance to his past inability. However, when he found me sweating profusely in the scorching heat of the sun, he immediately purchased one and connected it over my bed. What he could not do for his own father, he was bound to do for my comfort. I was often suffering from fever. He used to sit sleepless beside the sick bed the whole night and monitor the degree of my temperature in thermometer. Not only that, he also used to jot down all the details of my illness very carefully. When he met the doctor, he used to convey him each minute detail. The doctor did not have the patience to listen all those detailed information. In that case he would note down the details in a letter and hand it over to the doctor. He would plead before the Almighty and the departed souls of his parents to bless me to recover from my sickness. Once when I was in Std. VIII, I suffered from jaundice and was prone to vomit for 15 to 17 times in a day. My belly was totally empty, unable to hold even a little water. He sold all his landed property and mentally prepared himself for my treatment. I was just an ordinary boy, an unworthy and gullible fellow. I was neither good at studies nor able to handle any household work and also not able to help anyone in any means. I was totally useless, just nothing. I had no virtues and no talent. But why was father nurturing me with the dignity of a prince?

I had to go to Bargarh for completing my graduation. My father instructed my elder brother Manoranjan, the son of my aunt, to build a latrine especially for me. Brother Manoranjan, who loved me more than his younger brother, used to take out water from the well and fill the buckets for my bath. Wherever I needed to go, father reserved a car for my comfortable journey. Similarly, during my college days he reserved a car and took me on excursion to Puri, Konark, Nandankanan, Khandagiri and Udayagiri. He deliberately planned all tours during day time to let me enjoy the roadside trees, birds, animals, natural sights as well as the vast blue sky. During our return journey, he would instruct the driver to follow a different route so that I could see new sights and enjoy more.

My father was not satisfied only in rearing me up in an aristocratic style, rather he wanted me to follow the path paved by the great writers. He was the grandson of Swabhaba Kabi Gangadhar Meher and thus an ardent reader and silent worshipper of literature. He used to read literature without the knowledge of general public. It was he who used to connect my mind with the souls of poets like Gangadhar, Radhanath, Madhusudan and Nandakishor in an engrossed mood. May it be the creations of Rabindranath, Saratchandra, Bibhutibhushan Bandyopadhyay or Jesus Christ or Ramakrishna Paramahamsa or Vivekananda, he used to read all their sermons and lessons repeatedly and loudly for me. He used to express his frivolous dissatisfaction towards me as I could not read all the important books. To make me compensate the loss, he used to read aloud the important ideas and subject matters of different books. He also used to underline the valid points in a pen or pencil and keep it safely for me to read in future, even after his death.

My father knew that my little heart could not uphold the magnanimous ideologies and experiences on which he often emphasized. Nevertheless, sometimes he went on speaking the life story of Mahatma Gandhi, sometimes the philosophy of Vinoba Bhave and some other time the writings of Pearl S. Buck with deep admiration.

Many a times, I used to argue with him. He would listen to my arguments patiently and answer me affectionately. Once I asked him, "Father, if I love, care and respect those persons whom you don't love and from whom you have distanced yourself as you consider them to be people of evil character, will you be able to accept me?" This question was unexpected and it brought a drastic change in the facial expression of my father. He told in a mild anger, "Then I'll lose faith on you". After this he went to the toilet. But when he came back, he was found completely in a different mood. He rejected his own statement. Reflecting a bright smile on his face he said, "Well, you can love all as per your wish. I'll not mind that."

My father knew how little the vitality of my life was. Yet, he was trying his level best to raise it to a greater height where it could be more expansive, generous and humble. Now when I brood over the matter, I can realize at what level father wanted to find me. Did I really deserve that? Was there no narrowness or aversion in me? No! Not like that. In spite of the presence of all sorts of meanness in me, he constantly wanted me to be free, to be released from captivation.

Father intended to provide me a comfortable, contented and beautiful life. But he never borrowed a single penny from others for my education. Sacrificing his own comforts and adjusting with limited resources, he used to save money for my nourishment. He was the author of essays, stories, letters and diaries but, instead of taking care of publication of his books, he used to extend money for the publication of my books. In those days "Ankur" was being published collaboratively by me and brother Manoranjan. My father used to fill up the deficit money for its huge publicity.

Whatever may be described about him, I am sure, it will still remain incomplete. If I write a book on him, the pages of the book will not suffice his matchless contributions. There will always be the scope to write more. In this way my father had dedicated himself to fine-tune and beautify my outfit, my life style, my conduct and above all my heart. Perhaps his life was focused on a single target that was - to nurture his son as an extra-ordinary human being. As I have mentioned earlier, I was not worthy of that.

My father never used punishment or terrorism as a tool to bring me to the right track. Once at school I was beaten by the PET teacher during game period. When the matter came to the knowledge of my father, he visited the school and requested my teachers not to give me any corporal punishment at any cost.

When I was in Std. VIII or IX, I used to go to the Cinema Hall alone. Once when I requested father to allow me for watching a second show movie, he did not deny. But when the movie was over and the Hall was illuminated, I surprisingly found father sitting just after two or three lines from the line where I was sitting. He suddenly rose from his seat and went out of the Hall. In this way father was always at my back as protective shield, oblivion to me.

Once when the Annual Function of our school was over, I was returning home alone. He suddenly emerged and accompanied me. When he came to know that I was companionless at school, `he was grief-stricken. Now at the age of 56 I can understand well that nobody could have been more intimate a friend to me than my father. I used to come back home at 9.00pm after my tuition classes. No guardians or parents were going to fetch their children. It was only my father who was accompanying me. But, along with me he could enchant the remaining students in the ring of his affection and made us cross around two kilometers till we reached the area of human settlement.

How attached he was with the Art movies! He often stimulated me to watch those kinds of movies. He bought for me books like Minabazar, Shishulekha, Baramaza, Janhamamu etc. By the time I was enrolled into university, I had the opportunity to read many Bengali books which he purchased from Calcutta. Our financial condition was very miserable. I was getting a meager salary of Rs. 700/800 from lectureship. Everybody in our family was quite hopeful that one day my job was going to be permanent under the supervision of the Government. There was also no alternative choice for us. However, father often made me feel relaxed by telling, "If you like to continue the job, you can continue, otherwise not. We'll be able to manage anyhow with the grace of God."

My father thought himself to be a millionaire and assured me to live fearlessly. That was the reason why I never felt the compulsion to continue my job. In fact, I often forgot that I was in a job. For me my job was the greatest penance of my life. I was getting extreme contentment in loving my students as my family members and instilling in their minds fondness towards literature and our culture. When my students addressed me as "Sir", my heart was enveloped with an untold satisfaction. When I saw their lips blossomed with smile, a new life germinated in me. I was dedicated to my job considering it to be my real service to mankind. It was the end-product of the values and ethics my father had implanted in me. Though I was getting a meager salary, I felt as if my treasury was filled with thousand pieces of gem and pearl. Father never opposed my exuberant love towards my students; rather he motivated me constantly to love them selflessly.

Therefore, I was going to the college with the elegance of a millionaire's son. At the time of need I helped my students even financially as a result my students thought that I was not having any financial constraint. I never express myself as a poor man before my students. But I was incessantly inspired by my venerated father to continue my humbleness.

Today, I can feel very well the emotions of my father in Rabindranath's character Raicharan. What Raicharan did in his life, must have been understood by the sensitive readers of that story. He nourished his son with all the provisions and luxuries of a sophisticated family and when his son stepped into his youth, he surrendered him at the feet of his master. He confessed before the wife of his master that he had stolen the child that day from the bank of Padma and kept with him years together. Surprisingly, after losing Khokha Babu, Anukul Babu and his wife had not been blessed with any other child. Being broken-hearted at the irreparable loss of their only son, the couple was lost in utter darkness and depression. In the mean time, the return of Khokha Babu had brought an unexpected relief and exhilaration in the mind of the couple. There was not the slightest sign of poverty either on the face or on the body of that young boy. The couple was sure that such a handsome boy could never be of Raicharan. The couple could not restrain their emotion towards that boy. They thought, "Why should an old servant deceive his master?" They believed in the words of Raicharan. What he did was really inexcusable. For that reason the wife of Anukul Babu was still unhappy and rude towards him. Raicharan fell at the feet of his master and said, "I've not done anything. God has done. It was that invisible power, my destiny that prompted me to do everything". Standing in front of Anukul Babu and his wife, the boy immediately realized that they were his real parents because he had been brought up by Raicharan from his infancy till that date as if he was the son of his master and not at all as his own son. The boy also found Raicharan to be guilty of deceiving his master and keeping him away from his son. Raicharan did not speak a single word. He had a glance at his son for the last time. He touched the feet of his master and with a folding palm took farewell from everyone. After that he got mixed and lost in the vast population of the earth.

I know well why this Raicharan reared up his own son as the son of his master. The readers of this story also know the truth. AS an avid reader of Rabindranath, my father also knew the great sacrifice of Raicharan.

My father did not want to keep me away from his eyes even for a moment. Once I was tenacious to go to Sonepur to attend the marriage of sister Manorama. Father permitted me ultimately in tearful eyes. Wherever and whenever I went, I remember how he was waiting for my retreat in thirsty eyes; how he was praying God again and again for my safe retreat. He could not get relief till he saw me in his own eyes. Unfortunately, from the last fourteen years father has left me alone with mother and has departed to that world from which nobody ever returns. When I usually discussed about father with mother, she would express the delicate traits of father's character and say with intense love and consolation, "Don't worry. Wherever your father might be, he is always praying for your wellbeing". Such a statement of mother made my heart overflow with emotion. It filled my eyes with tears of happiness and I lost myself in the thoughts of my father silently.

Well, after reading the story of Rabindranath, I want to ask father a crucial question today. If he had been alive today, I must have asked him this question directly. Anyways, wherever and in whatever condition he may be, I want to ask him, "Father, please emerge once at least in my dream and tell me why you brought me up as a prince from my infancy to youth despite adverse financial constraints. Raicharan had lost the son of his master. So to compensate the loss, he brought up his own son as a prince and surrendered him at last at the feet of his master. But how can that be applicable to me? After all I am your own son. You had never lost anyone for your negligence. Unlike Raicharan, you had never been the cause of creating pain of separation in the heart of anyone. Then why father ….. why did you bring me up in an ambience of aristocracy? Tell me just once father, who was your master? To whom did you intend to surrender me? Please tell, I beg you, please tell. I'll continue asking you this troublesome question throughout my life till I get an answer from you. Indeed, I can realize today, why you were unable to establish yourself as a reputed writer. I accept that I have in myself a lot of evils, deficits and weaknesses. But, the truth is that I am your greatest creation. In whose name did you want to dedicate your greatest creation? To whom did you aspire to surrender me that you did not hesitate to endure so many afflictions and went on scattering the luminous light of animated happiness throughout your life?

O Dear Father! Kindly unveil this mystery and tell me the truth of your inner soul. Tell me your intension and sing once the song of peace in my unquenchable soul."

****

Encaged in your Love for Ever

My affectionate elder mother could not approve my request. Immediately after my request, warm tears started rolling down from both of her eyes. Each drop of her tears reflected the same scene. Today, I am going to narrate the scene which I saw in her tears.

Do you know what my request was? Just to keep a parrot in our house. The same wish had been ignited in the mind of my elder mother before four or five years. As I remember, it was my elder sister Mukta who had brought a beautiful infant parrot from the forest area. Thereafter, a new cage was purchased for the infant. My elder mother kept the infant in that cage with so much love and care as though it was her own baby. Every day she used to provide food to the baby in time. There was a water- bowl inside the cage. My elder mother was talking with the parrot very affectionately. For this reason the bird had forgotten its jungle as well as its mother. When it started producing sound, it addressed my elder mother as "Maa" many a times in a day in a sweet voice. After that there was no limit to the happiness of my elder mother. The marriage of her eldest daughter Mukta had been over. Her youngest daughter Indira was studying in high school. Sister Indira also became familiar with the parrot very soon. When my elder mother called her by name, the parrot was also imitating her style and calling her "Indira". When sister Indira came back home from school, the parrot was intimating everyone about her arrival by calling her name repeatedly. The parrot was the centre of attraction and a very lovable and familiar member of the family. It was not that I had not seen the parrot. But at that time I was too young to remember things. Of course, I have heard of the enchanting tales of the parrot from my elder mother so many times that I feel as if I see it in my own eyes, hear its addresses- 'Maa" and "Indira". My elder mother was exchanging her emotions with the parrot freely at her leisure. She was teaching it the mantra, "O God! Emancipate me from this birth as a bird". (Hey Chakradhara! Pakshi janmaru mate pari kara)

Who knew that the teachings of my elder mother would turn into a reality one day? Sister Indira was growing to marriageable age. Consequently, her marriage was settled very soon. A day was also fixed for her ring ceremony by the bridegroom's party. My elder mother never forgot her cute child, the parrot, however busy she might be. She used to serve in the cage hot rice and lentil soup as soon as it was cooked and ready to be served. The parrot, who was accustomed of eating hot rice and lentil soup, was always found in an ecstatic mood in its cage. Remaining inside the cage it was able to see all the family members, it talked with them and so never felt lonely. In this way the parrot had become an integral part of the family.

It was the ring ceremony day of sister Indira. That day a number of eminent persons, gentlemen and women reached our house from the side of the bridegroom. Obviously, my elder mother remained busy the whole day in the hospitality of the guests. My elder father, elder mother and other family members completed all the arrangements for their comfortable stay as well as the rituals of ring ceremony as per the social norms and customs in utmost sincerity. Finally they bid them farewell after the successful completion of the ceremony.

At the end of the ring ceremony all the family members seemed exhausted but still there was the mental satisfaction of completing everything as per expectation without any mistake. However, my elder mother suddenly realized the great mistake that she had committed on that day and her happy mood was soon converted into a mood of guilt and sorrow. What was that mistake?

My elder mother remained so busy in the hospitality of the home- coming guests that she had forgotten to serve food to the parrot in time. The moment she recalled it, she rushed to the kitchen and whatever was available there quickly collected in a bowl. Then she placed the bowl in front of the parrot in the cage and requested it to take the food. She thought that as usual the parrot would take the food immediately after it is served and be overjoyed. But it did not happen. She was shocked to see that the parrot did not touch anything. She came closer to the parrot and said, "O my child! I've committed a great mistake. I am grief-stricken being unable to serve you food in time. Please forgive me." She ventilated all her repentance and guilt before the parrot and begged forgiveness from it several times. She also patted on its back softly and requested it to take the food. But all her tender requests went in vain. The parrot seemed to say in tearful eyes, "Mother! How could you forget me? After being separated from my biological mother in the jungle, I had accepted you as my real mother. You loved me so much and I was also eagerly waiting for your cooked food everyday in my cage. But you forgot me today. How could you do that with me mother?"

The way a human child lodges frivolous complaints with the scarcity of the slightest affection from parents' side, similarly, the parrot seemed to complain a lot through its silent eyes and mouth. In spite of the repeated requests of my elder mother, it did not touch a single grain. In this way the day came to an end. The sun was set in the western sky. Gradually darkness entered into the house. All the stars in the sky started peeping at the sorrowful parrot. My elder mother was extremely tired. Nevertheless, she was coming intermittently to her lovable parrot to see if there was any progress in its behavior. However, as the night was growing deeper, her exhausted body refused to move an inch further and so she went to bed. Her eyelids were closed down spontaneously. But it was only for a short period of time. Her troubled mind could not take a peaceful sleep. During the night she suddenly woke up with a trembling heart and rushed to the parrot. Alas! She was extremely heart-broken to see the food lying as usual in front of the parrot, untouched and unseen and the parrot was standing silently with a bowing head. There was no end to the requests and repentances of my elder mother. But the parrot was absolutely motionless and nonreactive. Finding no other alternative my elder mother again proceeded to her bed with a warning that the parrot had to eat all the food by the next morning. She was quite hopeful that the next morning would bring a new beginning in her life when she would see energy and enthusiasm in the eyes and body of the parrot. The parrot was listening to the words of its mother without any response. Finally, my elder mother went to rest counting upon the faithfulness of the parrot.

Every morning my elder mother and sister Indira used to wake up with the frequent call of the parrot- "Maa"… "Maa"…. "Indira"….. "Indira". But that morning the house was utterly silent. The deep silence of the morning aggravated the gravity of the situation. My elder mother woke up with a start and straight came to the parrot to ensure its wellbeing. But….O My God! What she saw was unbelievable. She felt as if the soil under her feet was eroding quickly. Her ill fate had forced her to perceive that tormenting sight. The body of the parrot was lying in the cage still …lifeless.

I could see all those nerve-racking sights in the teardrops of my elder mother. I asked her, "What happened after that?"

My elder mother continued her narration. She attracted my attention towards a strange dream that she had visualized during her deep sleep that night. In her dream she saw the parrot, her endearing child. She saw her parrot instantly transforming into a beautiful fairy. The fairy said to her, "Mother! You always taught me to pray God to emancipate me from the body of a bird. I am actually a fairy of the Nandanvan of the heaven. I descended to the earth in the form of a bird to avail your love and affection. But now I have come back to my original habitat. Look at me. I am happy that God has approved my prayer and liberated me. You never feel that you have lost me. Don't be upset. Don't shed your pearl-like tears in my memory. You can always feel my presence in your heart. I can understand that for all the family members it was a grand day of celebration that day. But the truth is that each day was a day of celebration for me when I felt my importance in the family. When you look at me in warm eyes, when you pat on my back in your soft hand, when you offer me food with affection and exchange your feelings with me, when Indira shares her emotion with me so ardently, I get real pleasure of my life. However, that day I was deprived of the pleasure of celebration. So the little heart of this bird was filled with sorrow and gloominess. But today I am no more sorrowful. I am enjoying my emancipation. I have just one request for you. The cage in which I was living with utmost peace and safety should not be occupied by any other bird. Please allow the cage to remain empty forever in my memory. I am encaged in your love for ever- this realization has given me a rare experience of motherly touch."

My elder mother said to me gaspingly, "O my son! Never dream of encaging the birds in your entire life. Allow them to roam freely in nature. Let them enjoy their freedom. Let them spread their wings and soar high in the infinite sky."

As per the advice of my elder mother I did not request her any more to keep a parrot in that empty cage. I also uprooted the idea of encaging birds from my mind altogether.

I am fortunate enough to be able to see many trees with hundreds of parrots celebrating their freedom quite enthusiastically. I am unable to express how my heart fills with fascination and thrill at such sights. I often forget myself when I see them eating the ripe fruits from the branches of the trees. I am awestruck to see them fly under the blue sky in a group spreading and flapping their wings identically. They love the lap of nature. They love to float under the free sky. They equally love human beings. Once when I saw a tree full of parrots inside the boundary of the school, I could not find any difference between the students and the birds. The birds used to roam, fly and play in the school periphery and our students were perpetually exulted to find them in a happy mood. I personally feel that it may be the birds or the school students- all are connected to a bond of love. This multi-colored earth is a vast cage constructed by the Almighty and we are all imprisoned in it for ever bound in a common thread of love.

Can I ever forget that parrot of our house? It has been imprisoned in my heart's cage and remained alive forever.

Note- The heroine of this story is the eldest granddaughter-in law of the poet i.e the better half of Sri Purnachandra Meher. The title has been derived from Canto-4 of the classic epic poem "Tapaswini" in which Sita utters these words for Vana-Lakshmi - 'In your prison myself became a lifelong captive'

****

Mother's Fasting for Silence

I was probably at the age of nine or ten then. Once when I was going to my maternal uncle's house in Padmapur, I came to know about my mother's fasting for silence. Though my maternal uncle's house is in Padmapur, in reality the ancestors of my maternal uncle's house were the inhabitants of Gadvati. My maternal grandfather had permanently settled himself in Padmapur by constructing his own house there whereas his brother had settled himself in Gadvati. The distance between Padmapur and Gadvati may be 6 or 7 kilometres. At present a beautiful and noticeable straight road has been constructed to connect the two places but earlier when we were travelling through twisted narrow road in a bullock cart, the road seemed to be long and endless.

It was beyond my imagination that we had to travel in a different fashion on that long road on one occasion. That day after the sunrise, a beautiful bullock cart came and stood in front of my maternal uncle's house. I was not capable of knowing what kind of observation was going on in the house. I could not even ask anyone about that but I noticed that all seemed to be very busy and were ready to go to Gadvati.

My maternal grandfather and grandmother came out of the house carrying me. My mother was walking ahead holding probably a lighted earthen lamp and articles for worshipping God. The bullock cart was ready to set out for Gadvati. We all sat on the gunny sack widely spread in the cart. I lost my patience and asked, "Mother! Where are we going and for what?" I noticed mother for the first time in my life sitting in complete silence without answering my questions. My grandparents gesticulated me not to talk with my mother till we reached Gadvati.

The bullock cart stepped forward. I was nearly in tears thinking about my inability to talk with my mother. I gazed at mother's face in thirsty eyes. In her sitting posture with a vow of silence she was looking like an unattached ascetic.

After crossing the main road of Padmapur we moved ahead through an atmosphere which was enveloped with the scenic beauty of jungle. Many kinds of trees stood erect on both the sides of the road probably to console me. I lost myself in the greenery of the leaves. For some moments I forgot that I was forbidden to talk with mother. When I tried to initiate a conversation with her, my grandparents pampered me not to do so. It was a deserted area. I could hear the sweet sound of a cuckoo sitting at a branch end somewhere in the jungle. Its sweet tone was echoing throughout the jungle. Today, when I recall the event, I feel that the cuckoo was able to understand and accept my feelings and calling mother repeatedly through its cries. I also imagined that I was sitting in the thickness of the trees as a bird and in a soft and worried tone calling my mother. Moreover, even the abundant green leaves on each tree and the forest flowers available in some places could understand my condition and inspired me to tackle the situation calmly. I have rarely experienced such kind of solitude and silence in my life. My mother was silent. The vast blue sky overhead was silent. The wind was slow and soft. The trees, the roads and the very atmosphere maintained such an uncanny silence that amazed me naturally. I was also silent but only from outside. My mind was troubled from inside with a variety of questions - why my mother was observing fasting for silence. Why she could not pre-intimate me about it. At least she could have given me some hints........ and so on. It was impossible on my part to solve the riddle.

I was not very comfortable to travel in a bullock cart. My head was reeling and I felt like vomiting time and again. Nevertheless, finding no other alternative, I was sitting in it in absolute silence and great patience. Gadvati is the birth place of my mother. So naturally mother has deep inclination and fascination towards this place. She loves and remembers everyone. My younger grandfather, grandmother, Upendra uncle and my three aunts- all are very close to her heart and they have also abundant love and interest towards me. I have cherished the unique aroma of Gadvati in my heart till date.

The bullock cart was rolling ahead through the dense forest. It was probably after one hour that we entered the territory of Gadvati. The bullock cart stopped for a while. I saw the two bullocks that were tied on the front to drive the cart. I asked them the reason behind the silence of my mother. Though at that time I was not in a position to understand their language, but today, after crossing a long fifty years, I can understand their feelings. They were possibly telling me, "Dear Boy! We have been segregated from our mothers from the remote past. Thus, we have lost the fortune of uttering the word "Maa". When we grew slightly young we were attached to this bullock cart. Since then we are walking incessantly forgetting our sorrows and pain. As we too are deprived of the pleasure of calling "Maa", we are empathetic towards you." I looked at the four eyes of the two bullocks. They were shedding tears in silence. I also saw the mark of the rolling tears left on their cheeks which gave me a notion that they were crying from the time I started crying.

When the cart stopped for a while, my mother, as I recall, got down from it carrying the articles for worshipping God. She proceeded to a nearby pond and immersed the articles in its water. She also prayed the Almighty in folding palms and again came back to sit in the cart in earlier posture. After some time the cart stopped in front of my maternal uncle's house at Gadvati. All of us got down and stepped into the house. After that everything happened naturally. My mother started talking with me. She bowed her head in reverence of my younger grandparents. Nothing seemed abnormal after that.

At present my mother is living with me. But her mind is obsessed with the memories of our house at Barpali, Padmapur and Gadvati. She earnestly wants to visit these places and meet her family members but her physical weakness does not permit her to go anywhere. As my work place is in Balasore, she stays with me and always prays for me.

I want to ask her once why she had maintained complete silence without intimating me before half a

century. But sometimes I am confused whether to ask her or not as it is not in my control.

The night is getting deeper. From some days after taking food I am unwrapping the medicines and handing it over to mother as she cannot do it herself due to intense weakness. There is a separate living room and bathroom for her. If anybody of the family is absent from her for a longer period of time, that person is me only, her only son, the apple of her eyes. How contrasting it is! That day she had maintained silence for only around 1 hour but now a days out of 24 hours, more than 23 hours she has to remain silent out of compulsion. Her family members and relatives whom she often remembers live in distant places. Only I know how much worried I was that day for her silence of only 1 hour. In contrast, today due to my busy schedule when I cannot get the opportunity to talk with her, I cry like a child. It is needless to tell how much curious I am to run to her with her single call. I don't understand how to and whom to describe my utter helplessness.

Today evening I sent for a carpenter to our house. The reason is I want him to design a bench like narrow bed in my mother's room so that by using it I can stay with her, talk with her and even take rest whenever it is suitable on my part. I think that when I will be near her, I can ask her at a suitable moment, "Mother! Why did you observe fasting for silence during our tour from Padmapura to Gadvati fifty years back? Please disclose the mystery before me once."

I strongly believe that she will tell me the magnitude of fasting for silence.

****

In the Hope of a Phone Call

There are some people who immediately attract our attention towards themselves when we see them for the first time. In the same way, my attention was centered on him at the first sight. He was introducing books to the customers in 'Shantiduta' book stall during Bargarh book exhibition. I was looking at him ceaselessly. When he was demonstrating books to the book lovers, his face was illuminated with a smile as bright as the moonlight. He was dealing with the customers impressively not as a seller but as an intimate relative. His eyes were dazzling with the aura of light and I was restrained from taking back my attention from his warm smiles that clearly reflected a deep sense of belongingness. I wanted to go near him and be engrossed in a friendly conversation. But in that crowd the idea seemed to be implausible. As 'Shantiduta' had published my books, I wanted to ask him about the selling of those books. However, it was not possible to reach him in the throng. On the other hand, it was time to come back to Barpali, my native village, in the evening bus. So I came out of the exhibition reluctantly.

I stepped out onto the road from the fair but could not move much ahead. I felt as if somebody gripped my feet and did not allow me to move. I sensed the vibration of a pulsating tune in my heart. That tune pushed me backward. I could not go to the bus-stand anymore and surprisingly discovered myself near 'Shantiduta' book stall. I could understand very well where the source of that melodious tune was.

This time the crowd was slightly less than before. Taking the advantage of this opportunity, I went close to him. I asked about the sale of my book in a low voice. When he knew my identity, his facial expressions changed drastically. His eyes blossomed with the flowers of happiness. He greeted me joining his palms with utter reverence. The beauty of his personality, towards which I was frantically attracted before sometime from a distance, was reflected now on his entire face more deeply. It seemed that he had not learnt the skill of paying homage to the author of his publication house from somebody else; rather that was sprouting directly and spontaneously from his interior core.

I was amazed and asked, "What's your name?" He replied with a smile, "Sir, my name is Jayanta."

"You don't know Jayanta, how much you have amazed me. I was trying to leave this place but your behavior pulled me back." I told only this much but he was surprisingly thrilled with the touch of my words. He looked at me intently. Many more petals of Petunia fell down from his bright smile. Those petals could touch my heart in the form of his sincere devotion. "You're just like my father sir", Jayanta told emotionally.

I was also moved and touched with the sound of these words. The sky of our mind was splattered with the spectrum of rainbow colours.

I bade farewell from him that day but his image

started peeping into my heart constantly. So, before the culmination of the exhibition, I went to him once more. This time he was no more a stranger to me.

He expressed the jubilation of catching the moon when he saw me once more. I requested him to come outside of the stall and have some snacks with me. Initially he showed reluctance but being unable to avoid my earnest request, he sat with me later on. This time also I had to return to

Barpali. It was time to catch the bus. He accompanied me up to a few yards till we crossed the dark roads. In the mean time he collected all information from me about my family. He asked, "Sir, how many children do you have?"

Though it was extremely painful to give answer of that question, I had to do it for several times for several people. I answered him also.

He stopped at once. He was wonderstruck listening to my answer. I also stopped. With a suffocating tone he appealed, "Sir, promise me that you'll not tell like that from today onwards." I looked at him in questioning eyes and asked "Why?" He replied with love and intimacy, "I'm your son jayanta."

His words cooled down the fire which was burning my heart from the last fifteen years. The scorching heat of the sun was washed away with the ceaseless flow of rain. Some people speak sweeter than honey. My eyes were filled with tears. I could not speak a single word. I just gazed at his innocent face emotionally in that twilight. I wished I could embrace him and wet his entire face with the moist imprint of my countless kisses.

The wealth that I earned that day was shared equally with my wife. Her eyes glittered with tears of happiness as green leaves are enlivened after being drenched with the dew drops from the sky.

Whenever I went to Cuttack, I used to meet Jayanta in the office of 'Shantiduta'. During book exhibitions in Bhubaneswar, Sambalpur and Bargarh also I came across him. As soon as he met me, he would start complaining like why I was not making any contact with him over phone, why I had forgotten him, why I didn't take him home when he came to Bargarh and so on. I knew how his journey of passing +2 was full of struggle and how intensely he wanted to read in Barpali College under my supervision. However, I could not devote much time for him due to my busy schedules. For that reason he would swell with frivolous complaints. Though he was no more a child, but he would look pitiable and innocent like a child while lodging complaints. Just like Ramakrishna Paramahansa was rolling on the sand to get a few drops of love and care from the Divine Mother, similarly, he was in need of love and care. One day, he asked me, "Why don't you make a phone call to me?"

I answered, "I love to listen to your sweet complaints. That's why I don't ring you."

Indeed, I was mesmerized with a great sensation when he would open his complaint box. It was as sweet as tasting nectar. I often lost myself in it. He would scold me continuously in his appealing tone. He would say, "Why should you think about me? You don't need me at all. You have forgotten me totally, haven't you?"

I would try to console him. But the more I would try to console him, the more he would object.

That year there was the sad demise of distinguished Pruseth Sir who was just like my father. I went to the home of Pruseth Sir with my wife. I had to go to the book exhibition from there. When I informed my wife about the presence of Jayanta in the exhibition, she was also interested to join me. When we reached the book exhibition, what happened there was unbelievable. It added a new phase in our life. When he saw my wife, he expressed his deep feelings for her addressing her as 'Madam'. She was curious to hear that particular word which a motherly heart always wants to hear. Without any hesitation she said, "Jayanta! Don't call me Madam, call me 'Maa'."

These words of my wife made him tremble from head to feet. The most sacred Ganga does not flow only as a river; rather it can flow through the eyes in the form of tears. The eyes of Jayanta and my wife truly proved it. We discovered ourselves in a heavenly abode for a few moments.

The relationship between Jayanta and his mother grew deeper and deeper from that day. Now Jayanta started lodging the same complaints before his mother as he used to do before me. He would always tell, "I'm ready to go to Barpali if Sir is ready to accept me. When I could not talk with him over phone, he would say, "Sir has already forgotten me. At least you don't do the same."

Time rolled on. One day I received a telephonic message that the marriage of Jayanta had been fixed. I was surprised. He used to invite us repeatedly to his house but after the match was fixed, he insisted, "This time you must come with Maa."

In the mean time we were blessed with a son, our dear Ruru, good name Soubhik. After his birth it was no more feasible for us to meet Jayanta. When he was informed about Ruru, he said in his usual sweet voice, "Oh I see! Due to the arrival of my younger brother, you forgot me." We were both drenched with the glee and gratification of his transparent heart.

I wanted to invite Jayanta to our house at least once. At the same time, I wanted to visit his house too. I pleaded

God that I could meet Jayanta every year in the book fair.

But………. All of a sudden all my wishes got shattered. The Taj Mahal of my dreams collapsed. It was not believable. I was stunned with the sorrowful news. I was thunderstruck. Why should I believe in a heart-breaking news told by others? How could I bear my dreams to be devastated in a fraction of moment?

No…no….this is impossible. Now also I can hear his sweet voice…… "Sir, Namaskar. How're you Sir? How're all the family members? How's my Maa? Hope everybody is fine with the grace of God." These few words always gave birth to a new life in me. How can that life giving voice be silent?

Neither my heart nor my brain is ready to know how the accident occurred. I want to dial Jayanta's number instantly and I strongly believe that from the other side his sweet voice will come floating. He will surely tell, "Sir! You have forgotten me. You are not calling me anymore. Maa has also forgotten me." I am impatient and anxious to listen to his frivolous remarks and complaints.

……..Yes, he'll pick up the phone instantly…….

(Puja Issue of "Lekhalekhi" -2017)

****

Flowers of the Garden

I was in standard Six then. I did not like to go to school on the main road. People said that I was very bashful. When I was going through the main road, I felt that all the people present in the road side shops and houses were watching me only. I was utterly embarrassed. One winter afternoon when I was coming home during recess, I discovered a deserted road filled with red pebbles. From that day I continued using that road as my new way to and from the school. After I came out of my house, I used to cross a few crowded roads and then through that new road, I used to enter the school from its back door.

While going through that new road, I usually came across a round shaped grassy field just before reaching my school. I loved it so much that my walking pace used to slow down there and I considered myself as a free bird. The wind was blowing very slowly. To the north of that field there was a small hut and it never stood as an obstacle in my freedom. I had never seen anyone either entering the hut or coming out of it. But occasionally I could hear the pathetic and faint cry of an old lady. That sorrowful tune was weaving in the air and creating a vibration in that area.

I realized that the butterflies were flying with their colorful wings following that pathetic cry of the old lady. A bird couple in the nearby banyan tree was echoing the atmosphere with its chirruping. The cows and calves were grazing silently. The chameleon was nodding its head sitting on a branch end. A few patches of white clouds in the blue sky were igniting the pathos of my heart more deeply. The green leaves of the weeds were slowly swinging being absorbed in that sorrowful tune.

I would hear the sound with a calm and stable mind. Gradually when the sound fainted away, I would proceed to school. Some days during my return journey I would sit alone on the grassy lawn silently and reach home after the sunset. By that time I would hear that my grandfather had already come out of the house in search of me.

There was a small garden just nearby that hut. During the winter the whole garden was filled with huge yellow marigolds. That day each yellow marigold seemed more vibrant with deep yellow color when I found that a fairy like rosy little girl was playing in the garden amidst the marigolds. Her beautiful smile was mingling with the chattering of the birds.

I was involuntarily attracted towards the bamboo fence of the garden. When I discovered myself in a standing position holding the bamboo fence, I noticed that the fairy-like girl was standing near me and asking smilingly, "What do you want? Please tell."

I was startled all of a sudden. Then told fumblingly, "………er…...just a few flowers……."

The girl smiled gently and asked, "You want to take a few. What will you do?"

"Well…..need them for God"

"I'll surely give you some. Do you read in this school?"

"Yes. Why are you asking?"

"For nothing really serious. But why are you absent from the school now?"

I remained silent for the fear of my guilt to be exposed. She then repeated her question.

Finally I told the truth. "I am too much afraid of Mathematics class. Our Mathematics Sir beats us severely."

The girl laughed loudly. Her two long plaits started swinging in air. She was wearing a blue skirt and a white top. She supported me and told, "I am also scared of my Mathematics teacher."

I felt relieved.

"Do you sing?" She asked.

I was flushed. Then being unable to divert her request I sang a few lines.

She danced clapping her hands. Then I gathered courage and asked, "Very often I hear the cries of a lady in this cottage. Can you tell who is she?"

Just like a full moon is suddenly shadowed with a thin layer of black clouds, the pink face of the little girl turned gloomy. Her eyes were filled with tears. She uttered only one thing- "My old Grandma"

"Why does your old grandma cry? What happened to her?"

The small girl remained silent for some time.

I was also silent.

"She loves me so much. She cannot live without me. She is not able to see me at present."

"Why? Has she lost her eyesight?" I expressed my curiosity.

"No, she is thinking that I am not near her".

"This is surprising! I can see you are here".

I thought perhaps the old grandmother of the little girl had lost her memory or had become insane but I did not express anything.

The little girl wiped her tears out and said, "You wanted to take the marigolds, didn't you? Let me bring it for you."

Telling so she plucked a good number of flowers from those plants which her little hand could reach and after that filled my school bag with it. She questioned, "Will you pray for me one thing while offering these flowers to God?"

"Sure. What shall I beg for you? Please tell"

"I want God to make my grandma feel that I am always near her."

I returned home that day reiterating the request of the little girl. I shared everything with my grandfather. I also showed the flowers to my mother. I prepared a beautiful garland in my own hands and then entered into the Puja room for prayer.

My grandfather was very fond of children. Next day I went to school with much exhilaration remembering a few lines of my grandfather. My grandfather wanted me to ask that girl's name and also request her to sing a song. He told me that it was very indecent on my part that I didn't ask her to sing the previous day after I sang as per her request.

My mother wanted me to invite her home.

I proceeded keeping in mind all the requests of my grandfather and mother. I reached the garden and waited for a long time but there was no sign of that girl. Finally I went to school. On the way back from school I waited for the girl again but that girl did not turn up. I didn't feel inspired to go inside the cottage. I thought that I should meet her in the garden only. But it didn't happen. I waited there almost every day but returned home every day with utter disappointments. The sky looked deep blue every day. In the vast chest of the sky floated the light weighted clouds. The butterflies flew displaying their multi-colored wings. The grass looked green as usual and the chameleon nodded its head. The marigolds were singing in the slow breeze but I could not see that small girl playing in the garden anymore.

Frankly speaking, I was not a meritorious student. I had neglected my studies in standard six too. Gradually the summer came after the winter. My Annual Examination was over in April. I caught extreme fever during the summer vacation. As a result I could not go to school on the day of the proclamation of result. In my sick bed I said, "Mother! I've done very bad in examination. I must have failed."

Indeed, I failed in the Annual Examination of that academic session. One day, I went to school with my father for readmission. By that time the school had been reopened after the summer vacation. But that day Supplementary Examination was being conducted for many students those who had failed like me. It was the wish of my father that I should continue one year more in the same class and improve academically. But, as per the instruction of my teachers, I took Supplementary Examination. After examination I came back from the back side of the school. I saw that garden which was looking lifeless. The cottage was also lying in a dilapidated condition.

After some time I saw that an old lady was returning from her bath carrying a water-pot in her arm. She saw me and asked, "What're you looking at, child?"

Utilizing the golden opportunity I said, "Well,

Grandma! Can you tell something about the little girl who was present here…..?"

I was half finished and she interrupted, "Don't say anything about her, my child. She was just like a fairy. Her destiny had something else stored for her. She went to the other world leaving her old grandmother alone. It happened before two years. Her old grandmother could not tolerate the pain of her separation. She could not come out of her memories and passed away just last summer. For whom she could have lived! It was not possible on her part to live alone in this world. Leave it".

With a throbbing tone the old lady went on speaking all these lines at one go and proceeded ahead with a heavy sigh.

That day I suddenly faced a shower of rain on my way. I was completely drenched. Coming home I saw that the garland of the marigolds of last year was hanging in our Puja Room being completely withered. I fetched it and crushed it into tiny pieces. After that with the help of a spade I dug lightly a few patches of the soil in front of our house and sowed the seeds of marigold in it.

I asked my grandfather, "Shall we have a garden of marigolds this time?"

"Yes, yes - Why not", he replied very enthusiastically.

A few days passed in this way.

One day a teacher came and informed my father about my success in examination. Listening to this, I danced with joy and ran to the place of marigold seeds. I saw the tiny saplings raising their heads from the soil. My mind was filled with beautiful dreams. My interior core was exulted with countless possibilities of future.

Every year with the advent of the first rain, my mind is wet with a variety of dreams and thoughts. Every year we sow the seeds of marigold. The seeds are germinated, turn into saplings and the marigolds blossom. Amidst the beauty, charm and fragrance of the marigolds, I remember that little girl. I remember her sweet soft smile.

(Published in Bishuba Issue of "Prema" April-June 1987)

****

Sister Manaswini

When I recall sister Manaswini, her handwriting in each of her letters shimmers in my eyes clearly. If she had not come from Bhubaneswar to stay at Barpali, it would not have been possible on my part to know her so intimately.

My elder father (father of sister Manaswini and my father's elder brother) was working in the finance department of the Secretariat. When his whole family used to come to Barpali, it seemed to be the beginning of a grand festival. After staying one or one and half months when they retreated to Bhubaneswar, I remained speechless for many consecutive days from the very day of their departure. Most of the time, I was found sitting alone on a small cot in the courtyard of our harvesting field, the place where paddy was crushed and segregated. With the help of a small stick I drew a number of lines on the ground out of depression. At that time I had no idea that those lines were the tear lines of my broken and dejected heart. Today when I remember how I was gazing at the blue sky in my solitude, my heart is pounded with sorrow.

Those days of festivity used to pass smoothly in the company of all my brothers and sisters. But, when sister Manaswini alone came with my elder father, it did not cause a festival, rather it caused an atmosphere of exchanging emotions which was really extra-ordinary for me. She used to kid me telling that my voice sounded like that of girls even at my growing age. As there was much age gap between us, I usually remained suppressed before her. Therefore, she reached Barpali to break that boundary of suppression with the hammer of love. How can you know the actual reason behind her arrival to Barpali unless I tell you? The actual reason was that she had reached to a marriageable age. My elder father was worried about the infeasibility on the part of the bridegroom parties to go to Bhubaneswar to fix the match with sister Manaswini. So, he was inspired with the idea of leaving her at Barpali till her marriage was settled. There was a possibility that within 2/3 months of her stay here her marriage might be fixed with one of the boys who would visit our house with a marriage proposal. Sister Manaswini honoured the request of my elder father and for this reason came to Barpali leaving her parents, brothers and sisters in Bhubaneswar. After coming here she missed them a lot and shed tears intermittently. When she received letters from Kuni Didi, she became sentimental. Though I was her uncle's son, I was not less than her own brother. Why couldn't she realize that at that time?

It took some time for her to come out of that sentimentality and homesickness. Gradually she came closer to me. I also came very close to her heart impulsively. Sister Manaswini was the only girl among all brothers and sisters who knew Bengali. She used to read Bengali books and magazines which were read by my father and elder father. She used to tell me very often unforgettable stories in a poignant tone. It was from her that I heard the story of Kabuliwala written by Biswa Kabi Rabindranath Tagore for the first time. I was not that much good at studies. When sister Manaswini used to teach me, she seemed like my teacher and at the time of telling stories, she seemed like my sister. I was more interested in listening to the stories and real events of her own experiences than studies. She knew how I was doing in examinations. She was very worried about my performance in examinations. My elder father was a teacher in the high school of Barpali. So, sister Manaswini would tell, "If father had been here, your academic standard would have been better." This statement really touched my heart. Indeed, the presence of my elder father would have reformed me into a meritorious student. On the other hand, it is also true that if he had not gone to Bhubaneswar, he would not have been able to make my brothers and sisters highly erudite and civilized human beings. My elder father, brothers and sisters all wanted to take me to Bhubaneswar. But my father did not agree as I was his only son and sometimes my health condition was getting severe instantly.

Though I was in Std.VIII, I was considered to be very innocent, simple and pure-hearted like a baby by sister Manaswini. Every night she used to narrate me the stories of Hindi films. The story of "Do Akhen Barah Hath" is still fresh in my memory. If I go on speaking about her contents and unique narrative style, my narration will take a different turn and she will remain behind the screen. Therefore, I have decided to focus on only sister Manaswini instead of discussing all those stuff. Accordingly I have handed over my pen to my favourite student Darpadalana. While I am dictating those unforgettable memories of the past days to him over phone, he is capturing everything in his beautiful handwriting.

Sister Manaswini was accompanied by me to each place of Barpali that she visited. It was for her that I was

habituated of watching Hindi films. My mother, me and sister Manaswini used to go to cinema hall together. Now also I recall how profoundly we had enjoyed "Fagun". Gradually I did not hesitate to go alone to the cinema hall for a movie. The movies which were being watched by me at Barpali, had already been watched by sister Manaswini in Bhubaneswar. It is difficult to enlist how many characters, dialogues and songs of various films she has narrated to me. Her presentation of characters was so vigorous and vivacious that it left unforgettable images in my mind. I truly enjoyed her company. There were little openings on the walls of our store room upstairs. We used to pluck green tamarind secretly at night by inserting long stick through the openings. We had to complete this grand task very cautiously in order to avoid the attention of the people living nearby our house. After getting success in our attempts we were rolling on the ground with roaring laughter.

Sister Manaswini had not seen any cultivated land in Bhubaneswar. So we took her to our cultivated lands. At that time the workers were implanting paddy saplings in the cultivated plots. How enthusiastic Sister Manaswini was! She entered into the mud and started implanting the saplings herself along with other lady workers. We were not interested to come back from those green fields. I have no words to describe the taste of the home-made rice, cooked lentil and curry that I have taken in the company of my aunt, sister Indu and sister Manaswini sitting on the brink of the cultivated plot. I have never experienced that taste again in my life.

During sister Manaswini's stay at Barpali many people from the bridegrooms' side used to visit to our house for fixing the match. The responsibility of their total hospitality was on my shoulder. But the match could not be fixed so easily and the actual purpose of my elder father remained unfulfilled. Sister Manaswini could not stay at Barpali away from her parents and siblings any further. One day my elder father turned up at Barpali to take her back to Bhubaneswar. From that day the miseries of my life started. I was not ready to allow sister Manaswini to go to Bhubaneswar. If at all she went, I would also go with her- I remained stubborn in my condition and cried for hours together like a small child. Sister Manaswini touched the feet of my parents and took farewell when I was still crying.

The departure of sister Manaswini filled our home with a huge emptiness. That emptiness made me cry for many days together. When I remember those painful days of seclusion, I feel pathetic even today. Sister Manaswini sent a letter in which she wrote, "Little Boy! It hurt me when I found you crying glumly at the time of my departure."

She also wrote so many other things. After that she started writing letters for me and lovingly instructed me to reply her. As I recall I could write only one letter for her. So she wrote in jest "Little Boy! Are you going to write only one letter till you become an old man?" I roared with laughter after reading that statement. She further wrote, "Little Boy! Tell me whether the paddy saplings that I had implanted have grown up and loaded with paddy?" I have stored all her letters carefully. How beautiful her handwriting is! When she married and went from Barpali to Rourkela, her in law's house, she could send only one letter to me. She could not get time for the second letter being entangled with the family responsibilities. My face emanated sadness. It was only she who was coming to my memory lane again and again. I thought in jest whether she would write only one letter after her marriage till she became an old woman!

Alas! Indeed she grew old! All her happiness ended in a fraction of moment. She could no more wear colorful glass bangles around her wrists and red vermilion on her forehead. It was so agonizing to look at her empty and gloomy face. Who had got even the slightest idea that she was going to have such an unfavorable destiny? Who had thought that such a mishap would befall on her head so suddenly? The trumpets of her marriage are still ringing in my ears. But today the pitiable tune which is floating out of an invisible flute is ebbing out all my strength. Neither am I able to hear that tune nor am I able to console her in any language.

Only the Almighty and sister Manaswini herself knew how difficult it was for her to rear up her nephews and nieces. She had to endure endless pain and suffering. In spite of being the victim of poverty, she displayed unexpected courage and patience. Nowadays sometimes she stays in Bolangir and sometimes with her niece Rinki who has become a doctor. Sometimes she is also found with her youngest sister Buiee.

Today I am at the same place where sister Manaswini was living once, i.e the capital of Odisha, Bhubaneswar. Being a professor in the Department of Odia, I am working in Fakirmohan University, Balasore at present. This unworthy brother knows very well how he reached to this prestigious position. Whatever sister Manaswini had instilled in this incapable brother during her stay at Barpali, by virtue of all those stuff only today he has reached to such a height of success. It is true that he has not been able to achieve vast knowledge. But, if he possesses even a small drop of kindliness, that is similar to a small jasmine gifted by sister Manaswini. In spite of being so much unworthy if a boy like me can be a small firefly emitting the light of love, the credit goes to the charity of that person whose profound grace could enable Kalidas to sing the magnificence of Maa Saraswati, the goddess of knowledge. Just like pirate Ratnakara converted himself into pious Valmiki, she dispelled the termitarium of ignorance from me. The person who embellished my eyes with the collyrium of sympathy, she is none other than my sweet sister Manaswini. She is the sparkling particle of an electric line that can trickle matchless acumen in a simple and silly mind. For me she is a living image of Goddess Saraswati who is established in front of Vani Vihar. In the language of my great-grandfather "Phatubaba", the prolific creator of Odia literature, poet Gangadhar Meher, I want to dedicate and sing these lines for sister Manaswini in a forceful tone –

"Who art thou, O Lustrous Goddess!
with sacred radiant attire,
and with attractive tresses
surpassing the splendour of sapphire?"

The Goddess of sublime strength and knowledge, who is portrayed in the classic epic poem "Tapaswini" of Nature Poet Gangadhar Meher, had come to our house for some days in the guise of sister Manaswini and smeared her blessed hands on the head of her little brother being hypnotized with a divine inspiration. From that day the lustrous sister Manaswini has become a perennial source of stimulation for me. Today I want to address her, "My dear sister! Do you think I have earned enough knowledge? No, nothing I have earned. I am still the same silly boy of the past. I am still your incapable little brother. Tell me whether my tone matches with the feminine tone of that boy who was reading in Std. VIII?

(Published in the Autumn Issue of "Kahani" -2021)

****

My Old Teacher

I still remember clearly the day when I went to my old teacher for tuition for the first time. It was during the summer vacation after I passed standard three that I was asked to take tuition from that renowned and retired old teacher. Many of my classmates were taking tuition from him the previous year. For that reason I had a hidden interest to be taught by him. But the problem was that I was taking tuition from another teacher. So I was unable to express my interest for the old teacher before my father.

Father could read my mind. One day he took me to the ground floor veranda of a three-storey building of a rich man in front of his shop. As the rich man had sufficient rooms for his family, he had allowed the old teacher to conduct tuition classes on the ground floor veranda. The old teacher's house was in Gosein village which was adjacent to our village. That day the teacher was overwhelmed to see us. Leaving his seat he came to escort me and made me sit beside him very lovingly.

I was the centre of attraction for all the students present there. Everyone remained silent for some time due to my sudden appearance in the tuition class.

After answering to my inquisitions the teacher assigned me a question from Mathematics, a subject that I was least interested in, and concentrated on correcting the assignments given to other students. By that time the teacher's hair had turned entirely white due to old age. He had lost his front teeth. He was looking weak and wrinkled too.

I came to know about the presence of a tuft at the back side of the teacher's head when one of the students pulled it lightly with a chuckle. At that time the teacher was engaged in teaching English alphabets to another student. He did not show any reaction for that mischief. The notorious boy did not like the easy acceptance and tolerance of the teacher and pulled the tuft harder than before expecting a sharp reaction from him.

Now the teacher's fury knew no bound. He gazed at the boy with sharp eyes and said, "Look Sushil, this is for the fourth time today. If you dare to repeat it once more, you'll see what I am. I'll inform your father everything. Just wait and watch".

The boy replied with a daring heart, "Don't say anything. Not four or five times...... I'll drag your tuft hundred times." Another boy supported him and disclosed before everyone the proposal of Sushil's father to cut the teacher's tuft permanently. All laughed loudly. I also felt the urge to laugh but I remained silent. I was just astonished and shocked witnessing the whole scenario. The old man, being angry and dissatisfied with the laughter of other students, drew his attention towards me. He was happy and relieved to see my silent face and informed me about the regular insolent and unbearable conduct of other students. On the other hand, he recounted the glory and family reputation of my ancestors and anticipated that I could never behave indecently like the other students. Further, he prayed God to pave my path and bless me for inculcating decent and refined behaviour.

After a few days the boy who was pulling the old teacher's tuft more than anybody else and the boy who was supporting him both stopped attending the tuition classes. Neither could we know the reason behind that nor were we interested to know. One day we heard the old man grumbling with annoyance the misconduct of those students and their parents. A part of his infuriated remark was, "Intolerable!.....Ten times hair pulling for ten rupees!...... No need of that money.....Ten times!..... It is too much......" When he uttered these words in his toothless mouth, he was looking very dejected and helpless.

I was going to the tuition classes regularly. Our school reopened after the summer vacation. Accordingly, our tuition time changed from afternoon to morning along with the venue. In fact, the rich man had already instructed the teacher to leave that veranda as it was going to be let out. The teacher had persuaded the rich man to allow him to use the veranda only up to the summer. That's why when rain came, he had to leave the place. As per his ardent instruction we used to sing "Mangale aeela usha", a famous poem of Nature Poet Gangadhar Meher, in the morning before the beginning of the classes. I observed that when we were singing that song in total unison, he was listening to it quite passionately closing his eyes.

After a few days the old teacher had to leave that venue also. He had to shift to two other venues in a gap of fifteen days each. He was shifting us from one venue to the other as a cow-herd boy shifts his cattle from one grazing field to the other. Finally the veranda of a cannabis trader was selected for the purpose.

The cannabis trader had a fine rapport with Gosein village: may be due to his huge business transactions with the villagers or some other reasons. So our tuition teacher, who belonged to the same village, was also treated reverently by the trader and his wife both. We felt that they were also very sympathetic towards the old man. At times they used to share their happiness as well as sorrows with him. Even they used to consult him at the time of facing complex problems of life. The daughter of the trader, reading in standard one, also attended the tuition classes of the old man.

Every day the teacher used to reach the tuition venue in time. He used to cross the whole distance from his village to the tuition venue on his foot without caring for the scorching heat of the summer, the extreme rain and mud of rainy days and the low temperature of the winter. He was wrapped in a dirty half shirt and a thick dhoti. During winter season, he was found in an old and torn sweater with a grubby shawl to hide the holes on it.

Sometimes from the early morning he was fetching me from our house for the tuition. Of course for that he was demanding extra money from my father and his demand was always fulfilled also. One day when I was going with him, I felt as if he wanted to tell me something but somehow not able to tell. By the time we reached the veranda of the trader, no other student was present. I spread a gunnysack to sit and started my study just like a sincere and polite student. The teacher made a cursory glance all around and said to me in a shattered tone, "Dear Birendra, I am coming from the village from an early morning brushing my teeth in a rush. After that where is the scope to eat anything? Please lend me five paisa if you have. We'll eat puffed rice. Do you like puffed rice?"

It is important to note here that some days back the old man asked for five paisa to one of the tuition students but he denied on his face. When the scene was witnessed by the trader, he felt humiliated and insulted. Immediately he looked at the trader confidently and started laughing loudly. He tried to create an impression that he was simply kidding to know what was there in the mind of that student.

That day the teacher took five paisa from me. When other students joined the class, he gave the money to one among them to buy puffed rice for him. When the student brought it, he ate very contentedly. From that day onwards he went on taking five paisa from me every day. Both of us were quite accustomed to it gradually. There were some days when I was late for the class due to my laziness. By the time I used to reach, many other students were usually found occupying their seats and my teacher was found absorbed in teaching. Finding no other alternative, I used to sit beside him and initiate to hand him over "his claim" - five paisa. He used to spread his left hand towards me to receive it without disturbing his flow of teaching.

Some of the teachers of my school were also taking tuition classes but as a few of us were not attending their tuition classes, they were unhappy with us. The above mentioned incidents of five paisa somehow reached to their ears through some of my tuition friends. One day I was summoned by the head teacher. I went to his cabin. All the teachers of the school and all the students of the tuition class were present there beforehand. The head teacher asked me affectionately, "Is it true that the old teacher from whom you take tuition claims five paisa from you every day?"

-"Yes Sir".

- "What amount of money do you bring from home?"

-"Ten paisa".

Dinabandhu sir condemned the old teacher's very act of eating puffed rice with half of the money that a student brings from home for his personal use. He also gave a sensational speech on the good conduct of an ideal teacher. After that another teacher drew the attention of the head teacher towards the old teacher's wrong pronunciation of the letter "W" during the teaching of English. It was followed by a vigorous discussion on his dirty and careless get up and monkey-like appearance. Being active participants of this interesting discussion, some highlighted on how drops of his saliva used to come out of his mouth and sprinkle on the students as well as on their books and copies at the time of speaking. In short, all the teachers present in the cabin made the old teacher a laughing stock.

That day Dinabandhu sir took away from me a beautiful diary which I had stolen from the bag of my elder father. He advised me not to use such kind of valuable things at that tender age. I had also kept a one rupee note in that diary but no one knew it. When my family members inquired about the diary, I had to admit almost after two weeks that it had been stolen. Dinabadhu sir did not return the diary for many days. So finally my father approached him and demanded the diary. In spite of unwillingness Dinabandhu sir had to return the diary but that one rupee note was missing there. I sealed my mouth in fear of getting scolding from my father for committing another blunder.

We had no idea about the family of the old teacher. Some days his son used to teach us in his absence. He was an apprentice in the bicycle repairing shop adjacent to the bus stand.

One day when we just reached the tuition venue, we were surprised to hear the thundering roar of the rich trader and his wife coming from inside the house. Both of them eventually came out to the veranda together. The wife shouted at the old teacher, "We had thought the people of Gosein village to be very fine and honest gentlemen, but it is shameful that all the evil and crooked persons of the world are assembled here. Very bad....."

The old teacher's face looked almost dry and gloomy most of the time. Due to the bombarding words of the lady the remaining glaze on his face also faded away. He tried to manage his helpless situation and asked, "What happened madam? What is my mistake? Please tell me openly."

The lady mocked at my teacher and said, "All of Gosein village are crooked persons. How can you be an exception? We gave you our veranda only because you belong to Gosein village. If we had the slightest notion about the ill nature of the villagers, we would never have allowed you even to touch our veranda. You can't continue your coaching here from today onwards. Go to another place."

-"Please listen to me once. If I have done anything wrong, let me know about it. Why are you connecting me with other people of the village?"

-"No, no! In this Kali Yug the person whom you sympathize with, will sit on your head ultimately. We have done a great mistake by allowing you to conduct your tuition classes on our veranda."

The old man felt that his trouble was as big as that of a star which is lying isolated in the middle of the sky and going to be engulfed by a number of clouds rushing from all the four directions. We were just gazing at his miserable face silently and helplessly. We could not know the reason behind the animosity and frustration of the couple. Even till now I am unable to understand it.

The old man tried to pacify and persuade the couple in many ways but all his attempts went in vain. Finally, he requested a poor widow to give him the portico of her house for a few days for conducting tuition classes. Her house was being constructed with raw bricks. He assured her that he would make alternative arrangement and leave her portico within one week.

Due to some personal reasons I stopped attending the tuition classes of the old teacher that week only. After that I had seen him once or twice on the way in the same attire and appearance-dirty half shirt, a thick dhoti and a sunken face.

I can still remember two major incidents related to my old teacher when he was conducting classes on the portico of that building made up of raw bricks.

One day, I purchased two pieces of Rasagulla from a nearby hotel. My teacher said to me in a low voice, "Will you give me one out of that?"I offered him one piece of Rasagulla and he swallowed it with great contentment.

Ironically, Kalyani, the small daughter of that cannabis trader was still attending the tuition classes of the old teacher. One day he expressed his deep annoyance for Kalyani as a result she started crying bitterly. To our utter surprise, our tuition teacher also started crying with her being gripped with emotion.

After many years when I had already passed my graduation, it was my birthday and my father called me outside our house. I saw outside there was an old man standing with a cane. All his teeth had fallen. He had a hollowed and gloomy face. He was wearing a torn and dirty cloth. His eyes were sunken into the eye sockets.

When he saw me, his face glazed in happiness.

I suddenly recognized him. He was none other than my tuition teacher. He said in his toothless mouth smilingly, "My Boy! Will you not give me the Prasad of your birthday?" I went inside, brought some Prasad in a paper-bag and offered it to him. While eating the Prasad with satisfaction, he handed me over an old thick book.

The bunch of hair at the back of my teacher's head had turned entirely white and was hanging loosely as usual in spite of tolerating all offences and humiliation.

I turned over the first page of the book gifted by my old teacher. He blessed me patting on my head with his weak and trembling hand. An inexpressible flow of light splattered in my whole body at that time.

(Published in "Saptarshi" of March 1985)

****

Our Own House

Fourteen years had passed since Anurag Babu's marriage. He had been struggling to move ahead in the canoe of his life. He had shouldered the responsibility of four dependants at home. Being an ordinary clerk of the court, he had limited income with which he ceaselessly struggled to meet the high cost of living. While returning home from office, he used to visualize his unavoidable family obligations. Trusting on the divine gift of his two feet, he would come all the way home walking pleasurably.

With the approach of the evening, being drawn by the tie of filial affection, Anurag Babu hastened his steps. The moment he stepped into the house, Rabi addressed him repeatedly complaining, "The house-owner gave a good snubbing to mother in the morning. Have we not paid the rent, father?"

Shabi and Ranu listened to Rabi and they too repeated the same as a demonstration of their devotion towards mother. Anurag Babu unconsciously heaved a sigh of sadness.

"Father! If the house rent is not paid within four to six days, he has threatened to evict us", Ranu made it clear.

Anurag Babu heard all their complaints. He aimed at Asha Devi and remarked after a while, "As long as we don't have a house of our own, we have got to put up with all this. What else can be done?"

Asha Devi, who was bearing everything patiently, fixed her look on her husband hopefully.

"So we are going to have a house of our own, father?" Ranu wanted to confirm.

Anurag Babu became grave. However, the more he tried to conceal his inability from his children, the more it was disclosed. His face was covered with the shadow of depression.

He listened to Ranu and tried to give a smile. "Surely, we are going to have one", he gave the assurance.

Shabi asked, "Where is it being constructed?"

"I am looking out for a piece of land. It must be purchased".

"Father! Don't forget to make a reading room for me in the new house", Rabi entreated his father.

"Sure, all your demands will be fulfilled."

The entire family was at once engrossed in the dream of the new house. Turning her look to her husband Asha Devi said, "So we are going to build a house, isn't---- it----?"

"Yes, otherwise, how shall we manage Asha? We've put up with enough of troubles."

"Alright then, we are having a house. But you have to see that it should not be a huge one", Asha Devi suggested.

"Yes, I agree. Well, how many rooms do you think would be desirable?" Anurag Babu consulted her.

Asha gave a little thought to it and replied, "Is it five? Yes, just five rooms will do. No use having more rooms- a drawing room, a bed room, a store, a reading room and a kitchen... that's all we need. Latrine and bath rooms are bound to be there."

"Yes, the drawing room is to be nicely decorated with sofa set and a small table at the centre. A table-cloth with the flower vase made by mother will be there, just like the arrangement at Balabhadra Babu's residence, dear father", Rabi suddenly came forward with this suggestion aiming towards his father.

" Right. But the flower vase will look gorgeous if the

table cloth is a blend of black and white, isn't it so, father?" Ranu commented.

"Sure, sure, that will look very excellent Dear Mommy! But you have not mentioned the pictures to be hung up there." The eyes of Anurag Babu were filled with feelings of love and amusement both.

Rabi, Shabi and Ranu simultaneously started uttering the names of great souls.

"Well, My Kiddies! You are not supposed to mention the names all at a time. Speak one after another. All right Rabi! You tell what pictures are to be displayed?" Directing all of them to keep quiet, Anurag Babu proceeded further.

Ranu insisted on speaking first. Shabi complained that Rabi would mention the names of many great souls once he is given the opportunity.

"Very well, let's allow Ranu to speak first, Shabi will follow and I'll be the last," Rabi suggested.

"Yes, act accordingly. Don't make a scene unnecessarily. So, you had better speak out, Ranu," Asha Devi tried to convince her children like this in her soft tone.

Ranu's throat dried up while she could name none except Madhubabu and Gopabandhu. She had read about the said two characters in her text books. She appealed Anurag Babu to hang up the portraits of these two at any cost.

"The portraits of Fakirmohan, Radhanath, Madhusudan and Gangadhar are also to be put up there, Dear Father! They are the scintillating stars of Odia literary firmament. And, the photo of the World Poet –Rabindranath is sure to find a place there", Shabi furnished these names establishing over the ignorance of Ranu.

"See, Ranu and Shabi gave the names of poets only, Dear Father! We have to display the portraits of Netaji, Bapuji and Chachaji as well. It is they who brought freedom to our country," Rabi remarked.

When everything was heard, Anurag Babu concluded: "They are all bright stars of our country, isn't it so Shabi?"

Shabi consented.

Anurag Babu turned his looks to Asha Devi with a smile and remarked, "I can understand Asha, Ranu remembered the names of Madhubabu and Gopabandhu first. So, she'll be like them. And our Shabi will be a poet."

"And what about Rabi," asked Asha Devi.

"He'll launch a fight for the country, if necessary," Anurag Babu gave a brief comment.

Rabi, Shabi and Ranu were delighted to hear the prediction of their parents about their future.

"So, this is all about the verandah to the drawing room. To the left of it there will be God's room, bed room and store. To the right, there will be a reading room for children. Behind it there will be bath and attached latrine, "Asha Devi went on with the details.

While Anurag Babu was with all praise for Asha's plan, there was jubilation among all.

"And mind you, we shall have a small garden in front of the house in which there will be variety of flowers. We shall fetch water and pour it down the plants. Our children will be there to help us. We shall be seated there in the evening and talk to each other like this. And a boundary wall is to be constructed around the garden. How nice it will look!" observed Asha Devi.

"Sure, we shall build a home- a house of our own", suddenly they became conscious of their condition.

"Well, Asha! The night is probably far advanced. Have you got the food ready?"

"There was no rice in stock today morning. So I borrowed two "manas" of rice from Manda's mother to prepare food."

"Well, let the kiddies be fed", saying this Anurag Babu proceeded to the bed room. On the Verandah the three children made a roar for some paltry reasons.

To Asha Devi the heavy tone of Anurag seemed heavier.

****

Anhik's Reply

I did not receive his phone call deliberately. Why should I receive? What a hard time I had to face! Everybody knows with what difficulty I was rescued from that critical condition. Why didn't he ring me at least as a courtesy during that adverse time or even after that? It is difficult to estimate how many well wishers from all over Odisha prayed for my safe recovery.

Nobody can forget the devastating impact of Corona last year. I had never thought that I would be a victim of that deadly virus. Every day I was heading to my work place, my university, safely in my white car. Though being the Head of the Department I was discussing many things with a variety of gentlemen and interacting with my loving students and colleagues, I was always keeping a safe distance from all of them. I could not think myself insecure even for a moment. But in spite of all my precautions, I do not know how the virus infected me.

The day when test reports revealed that I was infected with Corona, I thought that by taking some medicines and remaining in isolation for a few days my temperature would come down. But it did not happen and my condition became critical gradually. First, I was taken to the Government Hospital, Balasore and then at midnight to Cuttack and ultimately I was admitted in KIMS Hospital,

Bhubaneswar. When I recall my miserable condition now, I start trembling out of trepidation. Those painful days that I had to spend in I.C.U, the untold suffering that I had to put up with due to the attack of the virus, can never be forgotten throughout my life. This sad news spread quickly through Facebook, Whatsapp and newspapers and reached to all my elders, well wishers and my dear students. I was not in a position to watch my mobile. In fact, mobile was not there with me. After being discharged from the hospital, I had to remain in a private hotel for about one month. At that time I came to know about everything from my son and wife. My heart was enveloped with utter gratitude towards all of them who expressed their care and concern towards me and prayed for my recovery.

How all these news could not reach to him! He could have made at least one phone call and asked about my condition. If that was also not possible, simply he could have left a short message for me. I admit that he is an innocent boy and I love him so much. In return, why couldn't he pray for my wellbeing even once? Suffering from such vanity I did not receive his phone call that day.

My meeting with him goes back to those days when I was working in Utkal University. I had been invited to adjudge a debate competition on behalf of a reputed institution. In that competition participants had to speak on the speech delivered by Swami Vivekananda in the religious conference of Chicago. Each participant presented the mesmerizing speech of Swami Vivekananda in his or her own style. I was listening to the deliberations of everyone quite mindfully. I was especially captivated with the delivery of a Std. VII boy who was dusky colored but with two luminous eyes, extra- ordinary facial expression and body language. I was astounded listening to his wonderful speech. It was difficult for me to discern whether the boy had entered into the spirit of Vivekananda or Vivekananda himself had emerged in the mind of that boy. It is needless to say that that particular boy secured the first position in the competition. After result declaration he touched my feet and sought my blessings. He stood before me in the most polite manner. I asked him, "What's your name?" He replied smilingly, "Anhik". It was a lovely name that could be easily memorized. He extended his small autograph note towards me. I wrote only one line in that note- "Anhik, you are really a small Vivekananda." This single sentence could create a thousand ripples in the hearts of him and his mother who had accompanied him. He noted down my mobile number. I also collected his contact number. Since that day I had been attached with him in an unconditional loving bond. Before going to participate in any competition, he used to take my advice and suggestion to improve his speech. Even he used to discuss with me his performance in various examinations briefly but with deep emotion. He considered me one of his pathfinders, one of his guardians.

When there was such a deep attachment and intimacy between us, I was slightly hurt to think that he did not make a single communication with me. Therefore, I did not receive his call instantly. Next moment he dialed my number once again. This time I received the call reluctantly. He greeted me with folding palms. I also duly replied him. I was sure that he would not ask about my health. So from my side I initiated the conversation and asked, "Anhik, how're you?" He was silent for some time and after that what he told made me feel extremely guilty. I thought that nobody could be more heartless than me in this world. The one sentence that he told was, "Sir! My father passed away in Corona."

All my grievances and false vanity melted away at once. I was shocked to know how easily that small boy spoke the bitterest truth of his life. Neither had I the strength to cry nor had I words to console him. My Anhik made me stand there speechless and motionless like a statue of stone. After that whatever I told him and whatever information I gathered from him about his utter helplessness and hard time, it is needless to describe here. I am not capable to describe also.

Anhik loved and respected me profoundly. He often sought my advice considering me as his guardian. After listening to his reply, I was converted into a completely grief-stricken and lifeless statue. I asked myself, "Can a heartless and incapable person like me be called the guardian of Anhik? Can I take the entire responsibility of a fatherless child? Is my heart which once filled with the elation of addressing him as "My Anhik", the same heart capable to carry the untold pain of Anhik's heart now ?"

From that day my throat has been choked. Anhik's reply has made me speechless.

****

Public Service

Man's calm and peaceful life is also connected with some sour memories that cannot be either ignored or avoided. Its image flashes in our inner canvas automatically and make us depressed and frustrated. I am still repentant of a particular memory of my life.

That day though the mini bus stopped at the station, there was no seat left. Nevertheless, some passengers were still boarding the bus. The helper was repeatedly shouting, "Hey! First allow the passengers to get down". However nobody was in a mood to listen to him. I also boarded the bus. After this bus there were many other buses in every half an hour or one hour but still I took that bus only. I had no specific work in that place where I was going. I could have gone after some time or even after two three days. But surprisingly I scheduled my journey that day only and in that particular bus too.

An old lady with unkempt hair, wrinkled skin and lean and thin body boarded the bus. Though all the seats were preoccupied and many passengers were standing, she looked around all the seats in her watery eyes. Then she sat on the floor of the bus at a distance of few steps from where I was standing. It was not possible on her part to stand in the line of other passengers.

The seat nearby which I was standing was occupied

by a gentleman. The gentleman said to the old lady, "Hey old lady! You will be jostled and trampled by others if you sit there. See how passengers are swarming into the bus."

The old lady pleaded, "Is the seat adjacent to you vacant Babu? Can I......."

The gentleman didn't wait for the old lady to complete her sentence. Anticipating the adjacent seat to be occupied by the old lady, he weaved his hand to indicate that there was no space for her.

I knew that the adjacent seat was vacant. After two or three minutes a gentleman in a white Khadi boarded the bus. The first gentleman smilingly allowed the second gentleman to occupy the vacant seat near him. Perhaps both were old friends who were meeting each other after a long duration. They remained engaged sharing their joys and sorrows with each other.

The first gentleman asked, "How long did you start wearing this Khadi?"

The second gentleman replied smilingly, "When we hear the news of countless poor citizens of our nation dying of starvation every day, will it be appropriate to live our lives in luxury?"

The first gentleman said, "Oh! I see. You are determined to devote your time in the service of the nation then. Very good! Very few people in the world are able to feel the pain and suffering of the poor. As you are a sensitive person, you are thinking about them. By the way, where are you going?"

The second gentleman replied, "To Bargarh. The

popular movie 'Kranti' is running in Uma Talkies. Don't you know? I am going to watch it. I think this movie contains all the ingredients to awaken the people from their deep sleep and come forward to protect the nation. Everyone should watch this movie. Of course, I could have gone for the movie some other day but today only I am going. And you?"

The first gentleman said, "Well, I am going to attend the birthday celebration of my nephew. Of course, it will fall after three days. So, it is not urgent to go today. On the other hand, I think it will be better if I go there two or three days before to help my sister in inviting the guests and making necessary arrangements for the party. As you know she is all alone and her husband is almost busy in court work. Anyways, what about you?"

The second gentleman said, "Life is moving ahead in a way. These days a committee has been formed under our initiative to render financial support to the poor. I have donated one hundred and fifty rupees to the committee."

The first gentleman thanked the second gentleman for his religious and developmental work. After that he went on describing the trials and tribulations of the poor of the present days.

The bus rolled on.

The bus conductor took bus fare from me and provided me the ticket. After that the above mentioned two gentlemen also paid the fare and received their tickets. Then the conductor asked the old lady to pay the fare. The old lady surrendered him the entire money that she had in her weak and trembling hand. The conductor counted it and demanded the remaining one rupee and fifty paisa. The old lady begged him, "Babu! I have no more money to pay you.

Please take me to my destination. My daughter has been hospitalized. I have to reach there today only. I'll save her life after reaching there. She has no money to purchase medicine. I'll look after her and save her life. I am her mother. Please have mercy on me and take me to my daughter Babu."

The old lady told everything breathlessly. By that time she had already dragged herself near my leg. I withdrew my leg instantly to avoid touching her dirty and stinky body.

The conductor did not believe in the words of the old lady. He became slightly angry and stated, "What shall I get out of your manipulative words? Alright, the vehicle will take you up to the distance for which you have paid the fare. I'll drop you on the way after crossing the exact distance."

The old lady requested, "For God's sake don't do like that Babu. Please take me up to my destination."

The conductor called the helper and instructed him to drop the lady on the way and then proceeded to deal with other passengers.

Time passed but the old lady showed no sign to pay the rest amount of money to the conductor. She rather pathetically requested him not to drop her half way. I felt that the lady was actually having no more money to pay.

There was enough money in the pocket of the second gentleman who had donated one hundred and fifty rupees to the committee meant for the wellbeing of the poor. Though he heard the pitiable appeal of the lady, he could not give only one rupee and fifty paisa for her. The man, who was sitting beside him, the first gentleman, was also a rich man. But both of them hesitated to help the poor lady.

I had ten to twelve rupees in my pocket. I thought to help the poor lady by paying one rupee and fifty paisa. I put my hand into my pocket to withdraw the money.

After some time the bus stopped in a small station. The helper ordered the old woman to get down. The woman was crying bitterly and pleading with folding palms to help her. But the helper had no time to listen to all that. He threw the baggage of the lady out of the bus which befell on the road. The woman once looked at all the passengers in her teary eyes and then got down the bus.

I heartily wanted that the old lady should reach her daughter and save her life. But I could not pay one rupee and fifty paisa to the bus conductor only for the fear of getting the attention of everyone and hampering their dignity at the same time.

The old lady had already left the bus. The bus rolled ahead. My hand was still inside my pocket.

(Published in the Magazine of Panchayat College, Bargarh, 1981-82)

****

Yakub

At last the heart of the truck driver was perfumed with the petals of kindness. For Amrit and Yakub it was like a heavenly refuge of father's lab. Their eyes marked tears of gratitude. The helper sitting near the driver was intimate to the owner of the truck more than the driver. Therefore, though the driver managed to move the truck, the decision of the helper was considered final in all matters. After getting the approval from the helper, the driver could make a small space for Amrit and Yakub to sit in the truck.

The truck moved ahead. Indeed, Amrit and Yakub would have reached their village in time. But the catastrophe that occurred on the way, made both the friends helpless. Both of them were the companions of village school and they had wretched family circumstances. The mother of Amrit had a premature death and the same happened to Yakub's father. Such common misfortunes and awful circumstances dragged them very close to each other. Amrit's father compensated the loss of Yakub's father by showering on him profuse fatherly love. Similarly, Amrit received motherly care from Yakub's mother. Both of them had diverse religions, yet, they realized that parents do not have any denominational identity. They are transcendental to all boundaries. They are just father and mother, epitome of selfless love and care. Similarly, friendship is also beyond the limitations of caste and religion. Though Amrit and

Yakub could not complete their school education, still they remained the most pampered sons of Mother India.

Amrit and Yakub had already sketched the road map to improve their financial condition. They joined an ice-cream producing factory in Calcutta as ordinary workers. They dwelt together, went to and from the factory together.

Yakub was suffering from illness intermittently. During critical hours Amrit was the only person available with him to look after him. It is true that a person having the wealth of nectar, can never feel the deficit of any other wealth in his life. Amrit used to give oil massage to the tired legs of Yakub. After sensing the ambrosial touch of his love and friendship, every time Yakub's sick body was energized with new life. Both of them were attached together with such an unconditional bond of love and friendship that their parents had nothing to worry about them. They were mentally ready to supplement their family income by shedding sweat together, devoting time in hard labour perpetually. They used to eat from one plate and exchange each other's garments. They had similar feelings and emotions. They emitted similar sweat and aroma. Their scentless garments were splattered with sweet perfume for them.

Nobody had the slightest notion of the quick invasion of such an epidemic to the world. Its name was Corona. Being the most contagious and fatal epidemic, it spread its poison all over the world. The news of the deaths of thousands of people everyday had made both the friends stunned and speechless. By reading Namaz Yakub started praying Allah to save mankind from the jaws of the demonic Corona. On the other hand, Amrit was an ardent devotee of Sri Ram. Amrit uttered the mantra -"Sarbe bhabantu sukhinah" in his morning and evening prayers. Sometimes Amrit read Namaz and Yakub read the Ramayana and Bhagavad Gita. The essence of both the religions had united the hearts of both the friends in a common thread. After being severely pleaded by their parents over phone, they were anxious. At last it was decided that they would come back to their village.

The total country was in complete lockdown due to the terrible consequences of Corona. Therefore it was not so easy for them to return to their motherland. Even so, both took a strong decision to start their journey on foot. It was the best pilgrimage for them as it was initiated with the pious intention of touching the soil of their motherland. Generally people leave their motherlands and move to far distant places for pilgrimage but during the acute spread of Corona pandemic, the affectionate call of motherland instigated everyone to liberate themselves from the distant places and move towards their most familiar and intimate homelands. Amrit and Yakub continued walking till their feet refused to move any further. When the whole world was trembling with the terror of Corona, both the friends went on discussing the unforgettable days of their infancy and childhood throughout their journey.

Now it was about to be evening. Amrit and Yakub noticed that a truck was coming from the rear side. Amrit beckoned his hand to stop the truck. After that he intimated the truck driver about their helpless condition. The truck driver looked at the helper, who was older than him and closer to the truck owner, in questioning eyes. First of all the helper did not agree to take them in but after listening to their polite requests and witnessing their wretchedness, his stony heart melted down and from it emerged the flowers of kindness. He gesticulated the driver to allow them to sit in the truck.

On the way without any prior intimation, the dark and dense clouds started spreading all over the sky with the flashing lightening that had the power to burn everything into ash within a moment. After some time, Amrit felt that his health was deteriorating. Yakub put his caring hand on the hand of Amrit and provided him constant support and consolation. In the mean time, the helper took a careful look on Amrit. He noticed that Amrit was no more able to keep a balance of his body due to excessive weakness. Instantly the helper asked in a rude voice, "Are you both Corona positive?"

These guys had no idea about the infectious disease-Corona. So, the question of the helper made them speechless. Outside there was a thick shower of rain and devastating hurricane and inside their hearts there was a deadly tsunami of pain and suffering. The helper instructed the driver to stop the vehicle at once on the way. Subsequently, he looked at Amrit and Yakub and said brusquely, "I suspect that both of you are Corona positive. In this circumstance we cannot take you with us any further. Get down here immediately." By this time Amrit had been pushed to the edge of the seat and he was about to fall down. Yakub was pleading with folding palms and trembling voice to at least take them up to their village road. Alas! None of his pleads was accepted by anyone. Finally dropping them in the middle of the road the helper himself started turning the steering wheel as he too knew driving. Within a fraction of moment the truck disappeared from the eyesight.

Of course, many other trucks passed through that road. Yakub urged each and every truck driver to take them up to their village but, none of them paid heed to it. Finally, Yakub lifted Amrit and carried him to the cool shade of a tree . By this time he was aware of the fact that Amrit was a Corona victim and it was not safe for him to be with Amrit. If Yakub wanted, he could go back to his village alone and protect himself from contamination but it was, indeed, beyond his imagination to leave Yakub helplessly there. Amrit was not only his best chum but also an equal partner of his sorrows and sufferings. How could he be inhuman to isolate Amrit at a time when he needed Yakub's support and help the most?

The tree was shedding tears which were rolling down through its green leaves. Amrit urged in a feeble tone, "Brother Yakub! Don't worry about me. Leave me here and proceed to our village in a vehicle. If I feel better, I'll certainly follow you in a different vehicle." Yakub had already pacified the storm of contradictory confrontations of his mind. This time he took the decision independently. He thought he could never leave Amrit alone at any cost. If he did so, how could he show his face to Amrit's father and his own mother at village? He imagined the helpless face of Amrit's father and remembered how he was told many a times not to isolate Amrit in any circumstance. The affectionate appeal of his mother too reiterated in his ears- "My Son! Never ever leave Amrit alone at any cost." Yakub was unable to discern which one was the pathetic voice of his mother and which one was of Amrit's father. Further, he realized the profound melancholy of Mother India that was dripping down in the form of tear drops from his eyes. He could not distinguish which stream of tears was descending from his own eyes and which one from the massive tree. Amrit's voice became gradually feeble. Yakub embraced his dear friend tightly. Then he lifted him to his lap and said in a wavering voice, "No, no Amrit, you cannot go away leaving me alone."

It was growing darker. Yakub could hear the loud noise of incessant rain from all corners. He could not differentiate between his pitiable cries and the cries of the incessant rain oozing out of the clouds that were wounded by the strokes of sharp lightening.

(Published in The Rhythm Eternal)

****

Mrs. Kalyani Panda is working as a PGT in English at DAV Public School, Chandrasekharpur, Bhubaneswar. She started her teaching career in 2000 after qualifying her Post-Graduation from Sambalpur University. Apart from teaching, she has a keen interest in singing and writing which she considers her two great passions of life. She was first inspired by Dr. Meher, her Odia teacher and the author of this book, to write articles for Basanti, the wall magazine of Barpali College. After that she continued her zeal for writing. During her 22 years of teaching career, she has written a number of articles both in English and Odia most of which have been published in school magazines and newspapers like the Instinct, Kusumayani, the Pioneer, the New Indian Express, Nirbhaya, Dhwani Pratidhwani and Nitidina. Having flair for writing, she has also edited numerous publications. She considers the blessings of her parents, teachers, family members and above all the Almighty as the real asset of her life.

Mr. Jayanta Kumar Mahattam, a multi-talented and fun-loving personality, has been pursuing his professional career as an Art-Teacher since 1999. He is an eminent artist, outstanding dramatist, versatile singer, instrumentalist, comedian and lyricist of Odisha. He is the recipient of Koshal Star Award as the Best Actor in a Sambalpuri CD film named "Bhalu Gadar Raja" in 2005. At present he is working as an Art Teacher in ODM Public School, Bhubaneswar. He is also one of the dedicated students of Dr. Manindra Kumar Meher, the author of this book. Dr. Meher's brain child 'Basanti', the wall magazine of Barpali college, was a conducive platform for many budding writers, singers and artists to exhibit their inherent talent and Mr. Mahattam is one among them. His artistic touch had enlivened many issues of 'Basanti' with colourful illustrations. He is indebted to his venerable teacher, Dr. Meher for providing him an opportunity to add charm and beauty to this book.

Black Eagle Books

www.blackeaglebooks.org
info@blackeaglebooks.org

Black Eagle Books, an independent publisher, was founded as a nonprofit organization in April, 2019. It is our mission to connect and engage the Indian diaspora and the world at large with the best of works of world literature published on a collaborative platform, with special emphasis on foregrounding Contemporary Classics and New Writing.

www.ingramcontent.com/pod-product-compliance
Lightning Source LLC
Chambersburg PA
CBHW020154120726
47903CB00007B/2559